THE SOVEREIGN FILES

THE SILENT ORDER

AGNITH J. BANERJEE

To the ones who write letters they never send,

To the dreamers who chase echoes of the past,

And to those who still believe in the magic of words—

This story is for you.

Contents

Foreword   *vii*

Preface   *ix*

Acknowledgements   *xi*

Prologue   *xiii*

1. Boarding The Train   1

2. Journey Started   4

3. New Country, New Murder   14

4. Secrets Of The Safe   21

5. Race Against Time   24

6. The Mastermind Revealed   28

7. The Web Of Deception   35

8. The Station Of No Return   39

9. Buried Secrets   49

10. The Architect's Truth   60

11. The Forgotten Son   64

12. The Black Archives   74

13. The Hunt Begins   82

14. No Safe Haven   89

15. The Revenant's Wrath   93

16. The Contingency Plan   96

17. Into The Lion's Den   102

18. No Room For Doubt   109

19. The Final Hunt   115

20. A Step Into The Fire   122

21. The Sovereign Order Strikes Back   128

22. The Final Battle Begins   133

Contents

Epilogue: Shadows and Echoes   139

Afterword   141

Foreword

When I first read the early drafts of The Sovereign Files, I knew this story was special. It is not just about murder and mystery; it is about the things in front of us, searching for them in the way we are and overlooking them, the way a letter, a single sentence, or even an unfinished word can hold a lifetime of emotions.

Agnith has a rare gift—making you feel deeply with just a few lines. As you turn these pages, prepare yourself for a journey that is as much about self-discovery as it is about the search for truth with Ahaan and Rohan. Their story will remind you that sometimes, silence speaks louder than words.

I hope you cherish this book as much as I have.
—Puneet Mehta

Preface

Some stories are meant to be told. Others are meant to be buried.

I never imagined how deep the rabbit hole would go when I began writing this book. What started as a simple tale of mystery—a luxurious train ride, a detective caught in the wrong place at the wrong time—soon unraveled into something much bigger. The Sovereign Order. A name whispered through history, a shadow organization shaping the world from behind the curtain.

At the heart of it all stood Ahaan Mehra, a private investigator who never asked to be part of a global conspiracy. But fate had other plans. A simple murder led to an all-out war against an enemy with limitless reach. Alongside Rohan, Esha, and Bilal, Ahaan was forced to fight against the unseen rulers of the world. They ran through cities, infiltrated compounds, uncovered secrets meant to stay buried. They weren't just uncovering a crime; they were exposing power itself.

This book is more than just a thriller. It's a glimpse into a world we don't see, a world where the ones pulling the strings don't want to be found. What if history was never what we were told? What if the ones in power weren't elected, but chosen in the shadows?

Volume I is just the beginning. A war has started. But the real question is—can it be won?

Agnith J. Banerjee

Acknowledgements

No book is ever written alone, and The Sovereign Files is no exception. I want to thank my friends for believing in this story and helping refine it into something truly special. To my beta readers, Puneet Mehta,Krutika Sanap,Vedant Thampi,Nishi Gupta and Renee Singh, your feedback and encouragement shaped Ahaan's world in ways I never imagined.

A heartfelt thank you to my family and friends, who tolerated my late-night writing sessions and endless discussions about fictional characters as if they were real.

And finally, to you, the reader—thank you for picking up this book and giving it a chance. Without you, stories would have no purpose.

Until the next adventure,
Agnith Banerjee

Prologue

Vienna, 1968

The candle flickered against the grand mahogany table, casting long, restless shadows upon the velvet-draped walls. A dozen men and women sat in perfect silence, their faces half-lit, half-hidden—an assembly of ghosts that had shaped the world in ways history books would never dare record.

At the head of the table, an older man in a tailored black suit adjusted his cufflinks. His voice, when it came, was cold and measured.

"The transition has begun. The old systems are crumbling faster than anticipated, and the world is hungry for order. Our order."

No one spoke, but a few exchanged glances.

"The Sovereign Order was never meant to rule," the man continued. "Only to ensure that those who do… follow the correct path." His gaze settled on a single figure at the far end of the table. "And yet, we find ourselves at a precipice. Certain dissidents have chosen to believe that history belongs to the people. That it should be free. That it should be… unpredictable."

A soft chuckle rippled through the room—low, knowing, predatory.

The man leaned forward. "That is why he must be removed."

Across from him, a younger man—sharp-eyed, calculating—met his gaze without flinching. He had been silent until now, but when he spoke, his voice carried an unsettling certainty.

"History does not belong to the people," he said. "It belongs to the ones who write it."

The room fell into heavy silence.

"Then it is decided," the older man murmured, nodding. "Kabir Mehra will erase himself from history. And in his place..." He let the words hang in the air, a ghost of a smile on his lips.

"A perfect successor will be born."

With that, the candle was snuffed out, plunging the room into darkness.

CHAPTER ONE

BOARDING THE TRAIN

1st March 1998

I sat on my couch, sipping a hot cup of coffee, when the mail arrived. Among the usual bills and letters, one envelope stood out—an invitation.

The elegant golden lettering read:

"Experience the most luxurious train the world has ever witnessed—The Kohinoor Express."

I stared at the words for a moment, debating whether I could afford such a journey. As a 27-year-old private investigator, I didn't exactly have a high-paying job. Luxury was a world far removed from mine. But the more I thought about it, the more I felt an undeniable pull.

"Why not?" I muttered to myself. "A once-in-a-lifetime journey through the heart of Europe. And besides, it's free to dream."

On the night of 4th March, I packed my bags. The train was set to depart the next morning from Delhi (India) to London (England)—a breathtaking 5-day, 4-night expedition crossing 13 countries: Pakistan, Iran, Turkey, Bulgaria, Romania, Serbia, Croatia, Slovenia, Italy, France, and finally, after crossing the English Channel, arriving in London.

Excitement coursed through me. A train that would take me across continents? This wasn't just a trip—it was an adventure.

Delhi Station – 5th March 1998

The long-awaited day had arrived. With my luggage and passport in hand, I reached Delhi Station in time for the grand inauguration ceremony. The place was buzzing with dignitaries, celebrities, and travelers from all walks of life.

At the ticket counter, I approached the man behind the desk and hesitantly asked,

"Bhaiya, how much do I need to pay for the ticket?"

The man smiled. "Sir, the journey is completely free for the first 120 passengers. You are number five on the list."

I was taken aback. A trip of this grandeur—for free? It felt too good to be true.

First Impressions

As I stepped aboard, the staff welcomed me warmly, placing a fragrant flower garland around my neck and handing me a refreshing drink. A well-dressed man named Nitin greeted me with a polite nod.

"Sir, I am your personal butler for this journey. Please, allow me to escort you to your suite."

Following him down the lavish corridor, I could feel my pulse quicken. The moment we entered my cabin, my jaw nearly hit the floor.

The room was enormous.

Two luxurious beds. A private bathroom. A personal balcony offering panoramic views of the landscapes we would pass. Everything about it screamed extravagance.

Stunned, I turned to Nitin. "What would be the cost of this room after the inaugural journey?"

His answer left me speechless.

"89,000 rupees per night, sir. Or approximately 2000 US dollars."

I swallowed hard. That was nearly two years of my salary. If this wasn't a free invitation, I wouldn't have stood a chance of affording it.

Meeting My Fellow Passenger

Just as I was absorbing my surroundings, I heard footsteps outside my cabin. My roommate had arrived.

Fifteen minutes passed before the door finally swung open. A young man entered, hauling a large suitcase behind him. I remained seated, engrossed in my book, as he settled in.

After a moment, he spoke up.

"Hi, I'm Rohan."

I looked up and saw a polite yet eager face.

"Detective Ahaan Mehra," I introduced myself, offering a handshake. "People call me the Sherlock of my town."

Rohan chuckled. "A detective, huh? This trip just got a lot more interesting."

He shared that he was a student from Kharagpur, eager to explore Europe. As we chatted, the sound of the whistle echoed through the grand station.

The Kohinoor Express had begun its journey.

And so, unknowingly, had the greatest mystery of my life.

CHAPTER TWO

JOURNEY STARTED

5th March 1998 – 10:00 AM

The Kohinoor Express roared to life, its wheels rolling out of New Delhi, embarking on its grand journey towards London. The excitement among the passengers was palpable—this was no ordinary train ride; it was a voyage through history, across 13 countries, promising an experience drenched in luxury and adventure.

Only a few hours had passed when an announcement invited all passengers to the Diner Cart for lunch. The clock had just struck 12:00 PM as Rohan and I made our way there, the aroma of freshly prepared delicacies filling the air.

As we settled in, my attention was drawn to two men standing near the bar, engaged in a hushed but intense argument. Their faces were tense, their words quick and sharp. At first, I dismissed them as just another pair of bickering travelers—perhaps drunk or simply disagreeing over something trivial.

Ignoring them, I turned back to my meal, unaware that this seemingly minor moment would soon become the start of something much bigger.

After lunch, we returned to our suite—a lavishly furnished space that still left me in awe. I switched on the television, letting the soft glow of the screen fill the room, while Rohan busied himself with planning our stops throughout the trip.

As evening approached, we stepped out onto the train balcony, watching the golden sun melt into the sands of Rajasthan. The sight was mesmerizing—miles of untouched desert stretching endlessly, kissed by the setting sun.

I felt at peace. But peace, I would soon realise, was only an illusion.

A Lavish Feast & A Familiar Sight

Exhaustion weighed heavily on me that day. As the train continued its journey through the night, I dozed off for a few hours—only to be shaken awake by Rohan.

"Get up, it's 9:30 PM. We need to head for dinner."

Reluctantly, I dragged myself out of bed and followed him to the Diner Cart.

The moment I stepped inside, I was left speechless.

The dining area was an extravagant display of global cuisine—Indian, Mexican, American, Chinese, Japanese, and more. The air buzzed with chatter, cutlery clinking against porcelain plates, and the rich scent of spices lingering in the atmosphere.

Rohan was beside himself with excitement. Over dinner, we discussed our planned excursions and realized that our itineraries were almost identical. To save on costs, we decided to explore together. It seemed like a practical arrangement, and I readily agreed.

After the meal, Rohan retired to our room, but I decided to take a walk along the train balcony, allowing the cool wind to refresh my thoughts.

That's when I saw them again.

The two men from earlier—still arguing, but this time, their words were clearer.

"The claim isn't valid unless the insurance policy is activated," one of them hissed.

"It was activated before the trip. Everything is in place," the other snapped back.

Their voices were low but intense, their expressions shadowed under the dim light. I didn't understand the details, but something about their conversation felt off. Before I could dwell on it further, one of the men suddenly looked up—his eyes locking onto mine.

His gaze was cold, sharp, calculating.

I quickly turned away and walked back to my suite, my heartbeat slightly faster than before.

The Mysterious Warning

Just as I was settling into bed, a sudden knock echoed through the cabin.

Rohan and I exchanged a glance. It was late—who could it be at this hour?

Cautiously, I approached the door and opened it.

Standing there was a small boy, no older than eight years old. His face was pale, his hands trembling as he silently handed me an envelope—then turned and ran away into the darkness of the corridor before I could ask anything.

A chill ran down my spine as I unfolded the note.

In hurried, uneven handwriting, it read:

"They will come after you. Be careful."

-Your Well Wisher

My fingers tightened around the paper.

"Who could have sent this?" I muttered.

Rohan scoffed. "Probably just some prank. It's late, let's not overthink it. We have an early morning—Tehran is our first stop."

I nodded, forcing myself to agree. But as I lay in bed, the words of the letter echoed in my mind.

"They will come after you."

Sleep didn't come easy that night.

And deep down, I knew—this was just the beginning.

A New Day

6th March 1998 – Morning Over Iran

I awoke to the rhythmic hum of the train as it glided through Isfahan, Iran. Through the window, I saw vast landscapes bathed in the soft morning light. A glance at my watch—340 km to Tehran. At a speed of 100 km/h, we would arrive in about three and a half hours.

Rohan stirred from his sleep as I greeted him.

"Good morning."

He stretched lazily while I ordered two cups of tea. As soon as we finished sipping, breakfast was served—fresh and steaming hot.

After eating, I stepped into the shower, letting the warm water wash away the fatigue. Rohan, meanwhile, remained by the window, admiring the passing scenery.

That's when it happened.

A soft knock on the door.

A small envelope slipped beneath it.

Rohan bent down, picking it up. The envelope was addressed to me.

I emerged from the shower moments later, drying my hair when Rohan handed me the letter.

"This just arrived for you."

I tore it open. My face drained of color as my eyes darted across the words. Without a second thought, I bolted out of the room, sprinting through the corridor.

"Ahaan! What happened?" Rohan called after me, running to keep up.

The letter had given me a room number.

I feared the worst.

And when I reached the cabin, my fears came true.

Inside, a gruesome murder—and a kidnapping.

A Crime on the Kohinoor Express

I immediately alerted the staff, who rushed in and sealed off the crime scene. The authorities in Tehran were informed. The Iranian State Police would be waiting as soon as we arrived.

By the time we pulled into Tehran, the station was swarming with officers.

The victim was none other than the Founder of the Kohinoor Express Company. His wife was missing.

My mind raced.

The two men from the bar... their whispered conversation about an insurance claim... Could it be?

Had they killed the Founder and kidnapped his wife to stop her from claiming any money?

I relayed this information to the police, describing the two men. The train was immediately halted, and an investigation began. A warrant was issued for the suspects, their descriptions plastered across the city.

The once lively train was now suffocating under an air of fear and uncertainty. Every passenger looked over their shoulder, whispers spreading like wildfire. Suspicion fell on me.

"Why is he always involved?"

The train staff stepped in, reassuring everyone of my profession.

"He's a detective. If anything, he's trying to help."

As the investigation progressed, fingerprints were recovered from the crime scene. They belonged to a man named Bilal.

The police launched a citywide search.

But what if Bilal wasn't outside the train?

What if he was still here?

As Rohan voiced this chilling thought, the train suddenly lurched forward.

We exchanged stunned glances.

"It's moving!" I gasped.

It wasn't supposed to.

The Tehran police had restricted it from leaving.

Which meant—someone had hijacked the locomotive.

"It's Bilal!"

I ran through the corridors, shoving past stunned passengers, until I reached the loco pilot's cabin.

The door was locked.

I slammed my weight against it—nothing.

Then, my eyes darted to the window.

Without thinking, I pried it open and climbed out.

The train had picked up full speed.

The wind roared in my ears, my heart pounding faster than the wheels beneath me. Clutching onto the railing, I edged sideways along the speeding train.

One wrong move, and I'd plummet into the darkness below.

With a final push, I leapt onto the locomotive's bogie.

My body crashed against the metal, but I forced myself up. I broke through the door—and immediately staggered back.

The stench of blood filled the cabin.

A dead body lay slumped on the floor.

Eyes—missing.

The skin was carved with deep, deliberate slices.

I vomited on the spot.

Pushing past the horror, I forced myself to the controls, slowing the train. But before I could fully stop it, a wave of dizziness crashed over me.

My vision blurred. My body collapsed.

A Night of Fear

I awoke to a sky full of stars.

A soft breeze caressed my face.

Groggy and disoriented, I looked around. The train had not stopped.

We had crossed into Turkey.

We were now in Diyarbakir.

Stumbling to my feet, I unlocked the door to the passenger bogie. A group of people rushed in.

"What the hell happened?"

"Why were you in there?"

A man spotted the body and recoiled.

"He killed him!" someone shouted.

"No!" I protested.

I demanded they match the corpse to Bilal's description.

They couldn't. This wasn't Bilal.

Whoever this was… he had similar facial features but lacked the distinctive scars Bilal was known for.

Something didn't add up.

I lit a cigar, sinking into a corner, numb from what I had just seen.

Never in my life did I expect to witness something so horrific.

The train's manager, Tejas, finally ordered a halt.

We were now stranded in the middle of nowhere—late at night.

"The cops will be here in the morning!" one of the attendants called out.

But no one slept.

Fear hung heavy in the air.

The thought of another murder loomed over us.

And now, I was no longer just a detective. I was becoming the prime suspect.

The night passed in terror.

CHAPTER THREE

New Country, New Murder

The first rays of the sun broke over the horizon, casting a dim glow over the train. Just as the night's fear began to settle, a gunshot shattered the silence.

We bolted from our rooms, rushing toward the sound.

The scene before us made our blood run cold.

Tejas.

The train's manager lay lifeless on the floor, a single bullet wound to his head.

The realization sank in like a stone—the killer was still among us.

And now, it was time to find out who.

The Turkish police, with help from their Iranian counterparts, finally tracked Bilal.

He was found hiding in the last carriages.

But something was off.

Bilal wasn't hiding because he was the killer.

He was hiding from Amir and Revant—the two men suspected of murdering the train's founder.

"They forced me," Bilal confessed, his voice trembling. "They told me to kill him... or they would kill me and my family."

It was a forced hand. He was no mastermind—he was just a pawn.

The police had no choice but to take him into custody.

But now, something even more disturbing became clear.

Amir and Revant—two of the most dangerous men on the train—were still at large.

I immediately turned to the Turkish police.

"What about Amir and Revant?"

"The Iranian police handled it," they replied.

That didn't sit right with me.

I called the Iranian authorities, demanding answers.

And their response made my stomach drop.

"Amir and Revant were arrested in Tehran for fraud," they said. "They were never on the train."

A cold realisation hit. The real killers were never on board.

The danger on this train was something else entirely.

For the first time in hours, the passengers breathed a sigh of relief.

But not me. There was still one loose end.

The train founder's wife was still missing.

She was last seen in Tehran, or so we thought.

"She must have been taken off the train," I murmured to myself.

But just as I settled on that theory, my phone rang.

It was Rohan. "Ahaan, come to the storage room. I found something."

I could hear the unease in his voice.

I ran. The storage room reeked of something foul.

The moment I stepped inside, I knew.

A rotting stench.

A puddle of blood on the floor.

Something hidden beneath a sheet.

My heart pounded against my ribs.

"No… please, no."

I reached for the cover, my hands trembling.

With one deep breath, I pulled it away.

And there she was.

A Revelation

The sight of the lifeless body of the founder's wife sent shivers down my spine. Her hands were tied, her face bore bruises, and there were marks around her neck, indicating strangulation. The room reeked of decay and fear. But something felt off. If she had been dead for a while, why hadn't anyone noticed the stench earlier?

Rohan and I stood in silence for a moment before we heard hurried footsteps behind us. A train attendant gasped at the scene and ran off, probably to inform the police. The Turkish officers arrived within minutes, sealing off the storage room.

Inspector Ahmad, who had been following the case closely, inspected the body and frowned. "She's been dead for at least a day, but look at this..." He pointed at a small, red silk scarf clasped in her stiff fingers.

"That looks expensive," I said, taking a closer look. "Could belong to someone onboard. Maybe even someone important."

Ahmad nodded. "We need to find out who owned this. And fast."

Rohan suddenly gasped. "The arguing men! One of them had a scarf just like this! I remember seeing it back at the bar."

We exchanged a glance before running back to the dining car, but when we got there, the two men were gone. A deep, sinking feeling settled in my gut. If they were missing, that meant they knew they were in danger—or worse, they had more to do.

"We need to check every cabin," I announced. "If they're still on board, they won't be able to hide for long."

The police agreed and a thorough search began.

As the investigation continued, another shocking revelation surfaced. The forensic team confirmed that the body in the locomotive— the one with missing eyes— was not actually an unknown passenger. It was one of the train engineers. His ID badge was found torn and hidden under his vest. That meant whoever had taken control of the train had posed as a staff member. But why?

Something wasn't adding up. The suspects Amir and Revant had been caught back in Tehran, yet murders were still happening on the train. That meant a different killer was on board, someone who had been hiding in plain sight all along.

Night fell once more, and passengers grew even more restless. Whispers filled the halls. I could feel their suspicious gazes on me, but I had no time to worry about that. I needed to figure out what was going on before another life was lost.

Then, just when I thought things couldn't get worse, the power went out.

The entire train was plunged into darkness. A few seconds later, the emergency lights flickered on, casting eerie shadows throughout the compartments. A scream echoed through the halls, sending a jolt of adrenaline through me. I grabbed my flashlight and ran toward the sound, with Rohan right behind me.

We found a woman standing near the bar, trembling and pointing at something on the floor. It was Nilesh—the butler who had first greeted me on the train. His throat was slit, and his eyes were wide open in shock. Next to his body was a bloodied playing card—the ace of spades.

"The killer is sending a message," Rohan muttered. "A symbol of death."

Then it hit me. "It's a pattern. The murderer is killing off people who are connected to the train. First the founder, then his wife, then an engineer, and now a butler. They're getting rid of people with authority or knowledge of how the train operates."

Inspector Ahmad looked grim. "That means we don't have much time before they strike again. We need to gather everyone in the lounge and question them one by one."

We did exactly that, assembling all the passengers in the grand lounge car. But as we were about to begin questioning, a chilling announcement played over the speakers.

"Ladies and gentlemen, I hope you're enjoying your journey. But this train is now under new management. If anyone dares to interfere, they'll meet the same fate as the others."

The room fell into a stunned silence.

A hijacking. The entire train had been taken over. But by whom?

Then, a sudden realization dawned on me. The founder's wife wasn't just killed—she was killed to silence her. But what if she had known something crucial? What if she had hidden something before she died?

I turned to Rohan. "We need to go back to the storage room. Now."

He hesitated for a second, but seeing the determination in my eyes, he nodded. We slipped away from the gathering crowd and hurried back. My heart was pounding as I examined the room once more, looking for anything unusual.

That's when I saw it.

A loose floorboard near where her body had been found.

Rohan and I exchanged glances before prying it open. Inside was a small leather-bound journal. I flipped through it, my eyes scanning the pages.

"It's the founder's wife's diary," I whispered. "She knew something."

Then, I read the last entry:

They're coming for us. The insurance was just a cover-up. The real secret is inside the safe in the manager's office. If anything happens to me, let someone trustworthy find it. There's proof of everything.

I turned to Rohan. "We need to get to that safe. It's the key to everything."

Little did I know, the true mastermind was already watching us, lurking in the shadows, waiting for the perfect moment to strike.

CHAPTER FOUR

SECRETS OF THE SAFE

The revelation in the diary sent a surge of adrenaline through my veins. If the founder's wife had known about something sinister, and if it was hidden inside the manager's safe, then that meant we were on the brink of uncovering something far bigger than just a murder.

Rohan and I wasted no time. We needed to get to the manager's office, but with the train under the control of an unknown hijacker, every step was a risk.

We cautiously made our way through the dimly lit corridors, keeping an ear out for any suspicious movements. The train was eerily silent, apart from the occasional rattling of the wheels against the tracks. Most passengers were still in the lounge, unaware of the secret we had just uncovered.

As we approached the manager's cabin, a shadow flickered at the corner of my eye. I stopped in my tracks and grabbed Rohan's arm. "Did you see that?" I whispered.

He nodded, swallowing hard. "Someone's watching us."

A loud crash echoed from behind, and we spun around, but there was nothing there. Whoever it was had just disappeared into the darkness. The air was thick with tension, but we couldn't afford to waste time. I reached for the door handle of the manager's office—locked. Of course, it was never going to be easy.

"We need the key," Rohan said, frustrated.

"Or," I replied, pulling out a hairpin from my pocket, "we improvise."

I bent the pin and inserted it into the keyhole, my fingers steady despite the pressure. Within seconds, there was a faint click. The door creaked open.

The room was in complete disarray. Papers were scattered across the floor, drawers had been yanked open, and the safe in the corner bore scratch marks, as if someone had tried to force it open but failed.

Rohan knelt beside the safe. "We need the combination."

I flipped through the diary again, searching for anything that could be a clue. Then I saw it—three numbers scribbled hastily in the margins: 031. A date? A code? It was worth a shot.

I punched in 031. The lock clicked open.

Inside, there were bundles of documents, but one caught my attention—a sealed envelope with the train company's emblem on it. I tore it open and my breath caught in my throat.

It was a set of confidential financial statements, along with a signed agreement between the founder and an unknown party. But the name that stood out was Amir & Revant Enterprises.

"They weren't just criminals," I murmured. "They had a financial stake in the train. They were partners."

Rohan's eyes widened. "But why would they kill the founder if they were involved in the business?"

"Because something went wrong," I speculated. "Maybe the founder found out they were laundering money or using the train for illegal activities. Maybe that's why his wife had to die too—she knew the truth."

Before Rohan could respond, the intercom crackled again.

"Time's up, detective. You've meddled enough. Now, let's see if you can survive what's coming next."

Suddenly, the train jolted violently, throwing us off balance. The emergency brakes had been disabled. We were accelerating.

And that's when we realized the horrifying truth—the train was on a collision course, and we had no way to stop it.

RACE AGAINST TIME

The walls of the manager's office rattled as the train picked up speed. Rohan and I stumbled, barely managing to stay on our feet. A cold wave of fear surged through me—whoever was controlling this train wanted us dead.

I grabbed the documents from the safe and stuffed them into my coat. "We need to get to the engine room. Now!"

We burst into the corridor, but the train was no longer silent. Panic had taken over. People screamed as they held onto whatever they could, trying to steady themselves. Dishes shattered in the dining cart. The lights flickered, adding to the chaos.

"Attention passengers," the intercom crackled again, the voice dripping with malice. "Brace yourselves for a rather explosive experience."

Explosive? My heart pounded. "Rohan, we're not just dealing with a runaway train. There's a bomb on board!"

His face was drained of color. "We need to find it—fast!"

We fought our way through the frantic passengers, dodging falling luggage and overturning furniture. As we reached the front of the train, a figure emerged from the shadows.

Bilal.

He was bruised, bloodied, and breathing heavily, but his eyes widened when he saw me. "You have to stop the train! They're going to blow it up before it reaches the next station."

"Where's the bomb?" I demanded.

"They... they hid it near the undercarriage, close to the front bogies," he panted. "I overheard them—there's a detonator linked to the speed of the train. The faster we go, the less time we have."

I exchanged a look with Rohan. "We have to get to the locomotive now!"

The doors to the engine room were locked, just like before. But this time, I wasn't going to waste time picking the lock. I grabbed a fire extinguisher from the emergency panel and slammed it against the glass. The door shattered, and we stormed inside.

The driver was slumped over the control panel, unconscious. Blood trickled down his forehead. The dashboard was flashing red—speedometers nearing dangerous levels, emergency brakes unresponsive.

"Rohan, check on him!" I ran to the controls, frantically searching for a way to slow us down. "Bilal, help me disable the throttle!"

The train lurched violently, nearly knocking us off balance again. Every second was precious. My hands trembled as I reached for the emergency override panel. I had no idea what I was doing—but I had to try.

Then, I saw it. Wires—too many of them. Someone had tampered with the system, rewiring the controls so the brakes couldn't be activated. The only way to stop the train now... was manually cutting the right wire.

One wrong move and we'd all be dead.

Bilal knelt beside me, sweat dripping down his face. "Red or blue?" he whispered.

I swallowed hard. "I don't know."

"Well, you better decide quickly," Rohan said, pointing at the dashboard. "Because we're about thirty seconds from derailing!"

I closed my eyes for half a second, thinking fast. They set up the bomb to detonate at high speed. That means the detonator must be wired to the main power supply…

I grabbed the blue wire.

"Wait—" Bilal started, but it was too late.

I yanked it free.

For a terrifying second, nothing happened.

Then—the train shuddered. The speedometer wavered.

And then, finally… we started to slow down.

The train screeched as it lost momentum, metal grinding against metal, sparks flying outside the windows. People screamed as they braced for impact.

Then—silence.

We had stopped.

A few meters ahead, a section of the tracks had been completely destroyed. If we had gone any further, we would've plunged into the ravine below.

I collapsed against the wall, my breath ragged.

We had survived.

But the mastermind behind this?

They were still out there.

And I wasn't stopping until I found them.

CHAPTER SIX

THE MASTERMIND REVEALED

The train lay motionless on the tracks, a stark contrast to the chaos that had erupted moments ago. Outside, a dense fog rolled over the valley, swallowing the wreckage of our near-disaster. Inside, passengers were slowly recovering, murmurs of fear and relief spreading through the train cars.

But my mind was far from calm.

Someone had orchestrated this entire catastrophe—hijacked the train, planted a bomb, and nearly killed everyone on board. And they were still among us.

Rohan helped the injured driver sit up. "He's alive," he confirmed, checking his pulse. "But someone knocked him out before all this started."

Bilal wiped the sweat off his brow. "Whoever it was, they wanted to make sure no one could stop the train."

I clenched my fists. "Then it has to be someone with access to the engine room. Someone who knew exactly how to sabotage the controls."

A voice interrupted from behind us. "I think I know who."

We turned to see Natasha, the train's head stewardess, stepping forward, her face pale but determined.

"I saw something earlier," she said. "Right before the train was hijacked. I... I didn't think much of it at the time, but now I realize I should have spoken up."

"What did you see?" I pressed.

She hesitated. "I saw Mr. Varma, the senior accountant for the train company, sneaking into the control room before the chaos started. He was carrying a small black bag—like the kind used for electrical tools."

Rohan and I exchanged glances. Varma. One of the men in charge of the train's finances. The same financial records we had found in the safe mentioned shady dealings—embezzlement, secret partnerships, and money laundering.

It made sense now.

If the founder had discovered the corruption within his own company, someone—perhaps multiple people—had decided to silence him. And when we got too close to the truth, they tried to silence us too.

"We need to find Varma," I said, standing up. "Now."

We moved swiftly through the train, scanning the shaken crowd. My heart pounded as I searched for any sign of the man in question.

And then, I saw him.

He was near the back of the train, quietly slipping through a door that led to the maintenance section.

He was trying to escape. "Stop him!" I shouted.

Bilal and Rohan bolted after him, but Varma was faster than he looked. He dashed through the narrow corridor, knocking over crates and tools to slow us down. But he wasn't getting away.

I launched myself forward, tackling him to the ground. He struggled, but I had adrenaline on my side. With Rohan's help, we pinned him down.

His face was contorted with rage. "You don't know what you're doing!" he spat.

"Oh, I think I do," I shot back. "You sabotaged the train, planted the bomb, and nearly killed everyone here. Now you're going to tell me why."

Varma's expression wavered. Then, he let out a bitter laugh. "You're too late," he muttered. "You have no idea what you've gotten yourself into."

A cold dread settled over me.

There was still something we hadn't uncovered. Something bigger.

Before I could press him further, a gunshot rang out.

I ducked instinctively. But the shot hadn't been aimed at me.

Varma gasped, his eyes widening in shock. Blood seeped through his shirt as he collapsed in my arms.

I turned sharply—just in time to see a shadowy figure disappearing into the night through the open train door.

The real mastermind was still out there. And now, they had just silenced their last loose end.

This wasn't over.

Not even close.

Shadows in the Fog

The sharp scent of gunpowder still lingered in the air. Varma's body slumped against me, his breath ragged and shallow. Blood seeped through his shirt, staining my hands.

"Varma, stay with me!" I urged, trying to keep him conscious. His lips parted, a faint whisper escaping before his body went limp.

I pressed two fingers to his neck. No pulse.

He was dead.

A cold dread settled in my chest. We had been seconds away from getting the truth, and now it had been stolen from us.

Rohan stood, scanning the darkened train corridor. "Whoever shot him is still on board."

I nodded, my mind racing. The killer had to be someone with a silencer—otherwise, the gunshot would have been loud enough to alert everyone on the train. This was a professional. Someone who knew exactly when and how to strike.

Bilal, still shaken, leaned against the wall. "We need to inform the passengers. There's a murderer still out there."

"No," I said firmly. "If we announce it now, we'll send them into a panic. The killer will use that chaos to escape."

Rohan's expression darkened. "So what do we do?"

I stood, taking a deep breath. "We set a trap."

The train's dining car was the most open space on board, filled with passengers still recovering from the near disaster. Some whispered anxiously, others clutched their loved ones. Every face was a mask of uncertainty.

But one of them was a murderer.

Rohan, Bilal, and I took our positions at different entry points of the dining car. Natasha played her role perfectly, stepping forward to make an announcement.

"Ladies and gentlemen," she began, her voice calm despite the tension, "we want to assure you that the train is now secure. However, we must request everyone to remain here until further notice."

Murmurs spread across the room. A few passengers looked nervous. Others exchanged glances. But I was watching for something else—body language, reactions, the telltale signs of someone trying to disappear.

Then I saw it.

A man in a dark grey suit, sitting at the farthest table, subtly shifting toward the exit. His fingers tapped anxiously on the table. His eyes flicked to the door, then back down.

I recognized him.

Rajiv Mehta. The company's legal advisor.

I approached, keeping my steps casual. "Mr. Mehta," I said smoothly. "Mind if I have a word?"

He looked up, feigning surprise. "Detective! Of course. What's this about?"

I slid into the seat across from him. "You seem a little tense."

He gave a forced chuckle. "Well, considering everything that's happened tonight, who wouldn't be?"

I leaned in. "You know, Varma was about to tell us something very important."

His smile didn't falter, but I saw the slightest twitch in his jaw. "Oh? And what was that?"

"That he wasn't working alone," I said, watching his reaction carefully. "That someone else was pulling the strings. Someone who just made sure he'd never speak again."

Silence.

Then—just for a fraction of a second—I saw it. A flicker of something in his eyes. Fear.

And that was all I needed.

Before he could react, I reached forward, grabbing his wrist. He tried to pull away, but Rohan and Bilal were already there, closing in.

"Let go of me!" he snapped.

"Not so fast." I reached into his coat pocket, pulling out a sleek black pistol. A silencer attached.

Gasps filled the room.

Mehta's face turned pale.

"I'd say this proves your involvement," I murmured.

He swallowed hard, his mask of confidence cracking. "You... you have no idea what you're dealing with," he hissed.

"Then why don't you enlighten us?" Rohan said, tightening his grip.

For a long moment, Mehta remained silent. Then he let out a slow exhale, his shoulders slumping.

"It was never just about the money," he said, his voice barely above a whisper. "Varma, the founder, even the hijacking—it was all just a distraction."

My blood ran cold. "A distraction for what?"

Mehta hesitated, then looked around the room. His lips pressed into a thin line.

"I'll tell you everything," he said. "But we're not safe here."

I exchanged a glance with Rohan.

Whatever this was, it wasn't over. And judging by the fear in Mehta's eyes, the real threat was still coming.

CHAPTER SEVEN

THE WEB OF DECEPTION

A heavy silence settled over the dining car. Passengers watched with wide eyes as Rajiv Mehta sat rigidly in his seat, his face pale under the dim train lights. The black pistol with the silencer lay on the table between us—a damning piece of evidence.

Rohan tightened his grip on Mehta's shoulder. "Start talking. Now."

Mehta swallowed hard. His eyes darted between me and the gun. "You don't understand," he said, his voice hoarse. "It's bigger than you think."

I crossed my arms. "Then make us understand."

For a moment, he hesitated, weighing his options. Then, with a deep breath, he began.

"It started years ago, long before this train ever became famous," Mehta murmured. "Amir & Revant Enterprises—they weren't just silent investors in the train company. They were using it for something else."

I frowned. "Laundering money?"

Mehta let out a bitter laugh. "That was just the surface. The real operation? Smuggling."

The word hit like a shockwave. Rohan stiffened beside me. Bilal leaned in closer, his eyes narrowing.

I exhaled slowly. "Smuggling what?"

Mehta hesitated again. Then he dropped his voice lower, barely above a whisper. "Diamonds. Weapons. Documents that could topple governments. Whatever paid the highest."

My grip on the edge of the table tightened. "And the founder—Mr. Khanna—he found out?"

Mehta nodded grimly. "He discovered the truth six months ago. He wanted out, but there was no way they were going to let him walk away. He started gathering evidence, planning to expose them. That's when everything started unraveling."

"The hijacking..." Rohan said slowly. "It wasn't just a cover-up, was it?"

Mehta shook his head. "No. It was the final move in a carefully planned game. The moment Khanna boarded this train, he was already a dead man."

A chill ran down my spine. This wasn't just a case of corporate betrayal. This was something far more dangerous.

Mehta leaned forward, lowering his voice even more. "And now that you know, you need to be very careful. They don't leave loose ends."

I clenched my jaw. "Who is 'they'?"

A flicker of fear passed through his eyes. He glanced around the room, lowering his voice even further. "There's someone else on this train. Someone is watching us. I don't know who, but I can feel it. If I tell you more here, we won't make it to the next station alive."

A sudden announcement crackled over the intercom, making us all jump.

"Attention passengers. Due to unforeseen circumstances, the train will be making an unscheduled stop at Çamlık Junction. Please remain in your seats."

The intercom clicked off.

That station had been abandoned for years. Why were we stopping there?

I turned to Rohan. His face was grim. "This isn't a coincidence."

I turned back to Mehta. "We're getting off this train at Çamlık. You're coming with us."

Mehta's fingers clenched into fists, but he gave a short nod. "If you want the full truth, it's your only chance."

Suddenly, the lights flickered. Then, without warning, the entire train plunged into darkness.

A single gunshot rang out.

And chaos erupted.

Passengers screamed. A tray crashed to the floor. I ducked instinctively, my hand going to my belt, though I had no weapon to defend myself.

Rohan cursed, grabbing my arm. "Get down!"

A second gunshot. A third. The sound echoed through the train car like thunder. I couldn't see anything in the pitch blackness, but I could hear the shuffle of hurried footsteps—someone was moving fast.

Then, as suddenly as they had gone out, the lights flickered back on.

Mehta was slumped forward on the table, blood pooling beneath him. A bullet hole in his temple.

I sprang to his side, but it was useless. He was gone.

"Damn it!" Rohan hissed, scanning the room. "Where's the shooter?"

I turned sharply, looking at the passengers. Some were crying, others in shock. But I knew the truth. The killer was among them, sitting quietly, blending in.

Someone had just silenced Mehta.

And now, we were the next targets.

The Junction was fast approaching.

And whatever waited for us there... it wasn't going to be friendly.

THE STATION OF NO RETURN

The train hurtled forward through the night, its wheels screaming against the tracks as we neared Çamlık Junction. The murder of Rajiv Mehta had sent a shockwave through the passengers, and fear clung to the air like a thick fog.

I pressed two fingers against Mehta's neck, even though I knew it was useless. His body was still warm, but the light had gone out of his eyes. Someone had shot him in cold blood, right in front of us, and yet none of us had seen the shooter.

Rohan's jaw tightened. "Whoever did this is still here."

He wasn't wrong. I scanned the dining car, my eyes darting across every passenger's face. Some were pale with horror, others frozen in place, but one of them was hiding something.

Bilal took a shaky step backward, his hands raised slightly as if he expected us to accuse him next. "I—I swear I didn't see anything," he stammered.

A lie.

Nobody saw anything in the darkness, but the fear in his eyes wasn't just from witnessing a murder. It was the fear of being caught.

I grabbed his wrist before he could move further. "Bilal, who are you working for?"

His face drained of color. "W-What?"

I tightened my grip. "You knew about the smuggling, didn't you? That's why you've been acting nervous since the start. You know more than you're letting on."

Bilal swallowed hard, his gaze darting toward the door as if calculating an escape.

Rohan stepped closer, cutting off his path. "We don't have time for games. Either you tell us the truth, or we let everyone in this car know that you're involved."

Bilal's breathing quickened. The weight of the situation pressed down on him until finally, his shoulders sagged in defeat.

"I was paid to keep quiet," he admitted in a whisper. "They told me not to ask questions. Just to make sure the cargo was handled smoothly."

I narrowed my eyes. "Cargo? What's in it?"

Bilal hesitated, glancing at Mehta's body as if afraid the same fate awaited him. "I—I don't know exactly. But I've seen the crates being loaded at night. Always unmarked. Always handled by the same men—foreigners. Not regular passengers. I swear, that's all I know!"

Rohan exchanged a glance with me. If what Bilal was saying was true, then the smuggling operation was bigger than we'd thought.

But before we could question him further, the train let out a shrill, ear-piercing screech.

We were stopping.

Çamlık Junction loomed ahead, bathed in an eerie glow under the moonlight. The station was abandoned—no lights, no workers, no sign of life. Just empty platforms covered in vines and decay.

But as the train slowed to a halt, I saw something that made my blood turn to ice.

A group of men stood waiting in the shadows, their figures barely visible in the dim glow of the train's exterior lights.

They weren't passengers.

They were here for something else.

The moment the train stopped, the tension inside the car was suffocating. Nobody moved. Nobody spoke. The fear was thick, crawling under our skin.

Then, without warning, the doors slid open.

A gust of cold night air rushed in, carrying the scent of damp earth and rusted metal. The men outside didn't step in. They simply stood there, waiting.

Waiting for something—or someone.

I stepped forward. "Who are you?"

One of the men stepped into the light. His face was sharp, his eyes cold and calculating. "Detective," he said smoothly. "We've been expecting you."

A chill ran down my spine. "You know who I am?"

The man smirked. "Of course. You've been meddling where you shouldn't. And now, you've reached the end of the line."

His hand twitched toward his jacket. Instinct kicked in—I grabbed Rohan and shoved him to the side just as a gunshot rang out.

The bullet buried itself into the wood behind me.

Screams erupted inside the train. Passengers ducked for cover as chaos unfolded. More men began climbing onto the train, weapons in hand.

This wasn't just a hijacking.

This was an execution.

Rohan and I moved fast, ducking into the corridor as bullets shredded the walls behind us.

"We need to get out of here," Rohan hissed.

I nodded. But how? The train was surrounded, and our only exit led straight into the arms of the enemy.

Unless…

"The cargo hold," I said suddenly.

Rohan's eyes widened. "Are you insane? That's where they keep the smuggled goods."

"Exactly." I grabbed his arm and pulled him toward the back of the train. "If they're protecting it, that means there's something important in there. Something they don't want us to see."

Rohan hesitated only a second before nodding. We moved quickly, slipping through the panicked crowd, dodging stray bullets as we made our way toward the rear compartments.

The moment we reached the cargo hold, I yanked the door open and we stumbled inside.

The air was thick with dust and the scent of oil. Large metal crates lined the walls, each marked with numbers but no clear labels.

Rohan turned to me. "What now?"

I didn't answer. Instead, I grabbed the nearest crate and forced it open.

Inside, nestled between layers of protective foam, were rows of black-market weapons.

Silencers. Rifles. Ammunition.

And something else.

Documents. Thick files sealed in waterproof covers, stamped with official-looking insignias.

I picked one up, flipping it open. My stomach twisted.

"These aren't just smuggling records," I whispered. "These are government files. Classified intelligence reports."

Rohan paled. "They're selling information?"

I nodded grimly. "And not just any information. These are details about international security deals. Military blueprints. Nuclear negotiations. If these fell into the wrong hands…"

Rohan didn't need me to finish.

But before we could process it further, heavy footsteps echoed outside the door.

"They're coming," Rohan muttered.

We had seconds to decide. Fight or flee?

But then I spotted something in the corner of the cargo hold—an emergency exit hatch.

Our way out.

I grabbed Rohan's arm. "This way!"

We sprinted toward the hatch, yanking it open just as the door behind us burst apart.

Bullets flew past us as we leaped out into the cold night.

We hit the ground hard, rolling onto the abandoned train tracks. My breath came in short, sharp bursts as I pushed myself up.

The men were already spilling out of the train, shouting, chasing.

Rohan grabbed my arm. "Run!"

We sprinted into the darkness, disappearing into the ghostly ruins of Çamlık Junction.

But deep down, I knew the truth.

We weren't running to safety.

We were running straight into the heart of the conspiracy.

And if we weren't careful…

We wouldn't make it out alive.

The Shadows of Death

Darkness swallowed us as we sprinted through the ruins of Çamlık Junction. The air was damp with the scent of rotting wood and rusted metal. This place had been abandoned for decades, but now it was alive with shadows, danger lurking behind every crumbling wall.

Gunfire crackled behind us, bullets kicking up dust and debris. Rohan grabbed my arm, pulling me behind an old cargo container as a fresh round of bullets whizzed past. My heart pounded against my ribs.

"We can't outrun them forever," Rohan panted. "We need a plan."

I peered through a crack in the container, counting at least five armed men moving through the station, their footsteps crunching against gravel and broken glass. More were surely coming. We were running out of time.

I gestured toward a rusted maintenance shed at the far end of the station. "We get inside, find a way to regroup."

Rohan nodded, and we moved quickly, staying low. The shed's door was jammed, swollen with age, but with a solid push, it groaned open. Inside, the air was stale, filled with the scent of oil and mold.

There was little inside—a few rusted tools, an overturned workbench, and shelves lined with forgotten equipment. But something caught my eye: an old railway map pinned to the wall, edges curled with time.

"Look at this," I whispered, tracing a faded red line with my fingers. "There's a tunnel system beneath the station."

Rohan's eyes lit up. "If it's still intact, we can use it to escape."

Before we could move, the shed door exploded inward.

The force sent me sprawling, my ears ringing as a figure loomed in the doorway, silhouetted by the dim station lights.

It was the man from before—the one who had greeted me on the train, the one who had ordered my execution.

"Detective," he drawled, stepping forward, gun in hand. "You should've stayed on the train."

Rohan lunged first, knocking the gun aside just as the man fired. The bullet ricocheted, shattering a window. The two men crashed against the shelves, sending tools and debris clattering.

I scrambled to my feet and grabbed the first thing I could—an old iron wrench. As the man shoved Rohan away, I swung hard. The wrench connected with his wrist, and his gun flew from his grip.

Rohan didn't hesitate. He tackled the man to the ground, pinning him as I kicked the gun out of reach.

"Who are you working for?" I demanded, pressing the wrench against his throat.

The man grinned, even as he struggled for breath. "You're too late. The deal is already in motion. And soon... none of this will matter."

A chill ran down my spine. "What deal?"

His grin widened. "You'll find out soon enough."

Before I could stop him, his hand shot to his pocket. A small click echoed in the shed.

Grenade.

"Run!" I shouted, grabbing Rohan and diving for cover as the explosion tore through the room.

Flames roared behind us as we hit the ground. Splinters of wood and metal rained down. My ears rang, my vision blurred. But we were alive.

The man, however, was gone—either dead or lost in the inferno.

Rohan groaned, pushing himself up. "We have to move. Now."

The explosion had drawn attention. More men were coming. I grabbed the map off the wall and forced myself to my feet.

We had one chance to escape.

And it was underground.

The entrance to the tunnels was hidden behind an old maintenance hatch, half-buried under rubble. It took both of us to pry it open, revealing a set of rusted metal rungs descending into the darkness below.

I hesitated for only a moment before climbing down, my boots clanging against the ladder. Rohan followed, pulling the hatch shut behind us just as voices echoed above.

We dropped into an underground passage, the air thick with dust and mildew. The only light came from a dim service bulb flickering in the distance.

"Where do these lead?" Rohan asked, his voice low.

I unfolded the map, tracing the faded lines. "There's an exit about two kilometers south. If we follow this tunnel, we can reach an old railway yard."

Rohan nodded. "Let's move."

We followed the narrow path, our footsteps echoing. The tunnel walls were lined with rusted pipes, and the occasional rat skittered past. I kept my eyes ahead, pushing forward despite the growing ache in my limbs.

Minutes passed. Then something changed.

The air grew colder. Staler.

A sound echoed through the tunnel—a metallic clank, followed by footsteps.

We weren't alone.

Rohan held up a hand, signaling for silence. We pressed against the tunnel wall, listening. The footsteps were slow, deliberate. And they were getting closer.

I gripped the wrench tighter. Whoever was down here wasn't lost. They were hunting us.

Then, a voice. Low. Menacing.

"You shouldn't have come here."

My breath hitched. The voice wasn't unfamiliar. It was one I had heard before.

Stepping from the shadows was someone I never expected to see.

Not an enemy.

Not a smuggler.

But someone I had trusted.

"No," Rohan whispered. "It can't be."

Betrayal sliced through me like a knife.

Because standing before us, gun in hand, was Bilal.

CHAPTER NINE

BURIED SECRETS

The tunnel was silent, except for the low hum of distant machinery. Bilal stood there, his gun steady, his expression unreadable.

"Bilal?" I breathed, trying to process the impossible. "You were helping them all along?"

His lips curled into a bitter smile. "Helping? No. But I knew. And I kept my mouth shut. Because I had no choice."

Rohan took a step forward, fists clenched. "You sold us out. You let them kill Mehta. You nearly got us killed. And now what? You pull the trigger on us too?"

Bilal hesitated. "I don't want to. But you've seen too much. They won't let you leave."

I met his gaze. "And you think they'll let you?"

Something flickered in Bilal's eyes. A shadow of doubt.

I seized the moment. "You can still make this right, Bilal. Help us. Tell us what you know."

He exhaled, lowering the gun slightly. "It's bigger than smuggling," he said. "It's about control. Information. Power. The Sovereign Order is everywhere. And if you don't stop them now... you'll never get another chance."

A sound echoed in the tunnel—footsteps. More men were coming.

Bilal's eyes darkened. "They're here. If you want to live, follow me."

With no other choice, we ran deeper into the darkness.

The Oath of Shadows

Bilal's footsteps echoed against the damp tunnel walls as he led us deeper into the underground. His breathing was steady, his shoulders tense. He hadn't spoken since he told us to follow him, but I could feel the weight of something unspoken pressing down on him.

Finally, he stopped near an old maintenance alcove, his face partially hidden in the dim light of a flickering service lamp.

"This isn't the first time I've been down here," he admitted, his voice low. "I was brought here when I was fifteen. The first time I met them."

Rohan narrowed his eyes. "Who? The smugglers?"

Bilal let out a dry, humorless chuckle. "No," he said. "The Sovereign Order."

I felt a chill creep up my spine. We had heard the name before, but now, in the silence of this forgotten tunnel, it carried a different weight.

"They don't exist on paper," Bilal continued. "No records. No official ties. But they've shaped more of history than any government ever could."

I folded my arms. "Who are they?"

Bilal exhaled slowly. "A shadow government. A council of unseen hands that has guided the world for centuries—not through conquest, not through force, but through influence. They are not kings, nor politicians, but the ones who decide who rules and who falls. They control economies, wars, revolutions... and they do it without ever being named."

Rohan frowned. "And you expect us to believe they brought a fifteen-year-old kid into their ranks?"

Bilal's jaw tightened. "They don't recruit. They take. I was an orphan, living in the slums of Istanbul, stealing to survive. One night, I broke into a building I shouldn't have—an old bank, abandoned for decades. Or at least, that's what I thought."

His hands clenched into fists, as if the memory itself burned him.

"There were men inside," he continued. "Not just any men—powerful ones. They sat around a circular table, speaking in hushed voices. They had files on people—leaders, journalists, scientists. Some of those names later died in 'accidents.' Some vanished. Some became presidents and CEOs. I had stumbled into something I wasn't meant to see."

I exchanged a glance with Rohan.

"What happened next?" I asked.

Bilal's eyes darkened. "They caught me, of course. I was just a street rat to them, an inconvenience. I should have been killed on the spot. But one of them—an older man, dressed in a black suit—looked at me and said, 'This boy has no past, no future. He is blank. He can be written.'"

A shiver ran through me.

"That was my initiation," Bilal murmured. "They erased me. Took me in, trained me. They taught me languages, history, strategy. And when I was old enough, they sent me into the world—not as an assassin, not as a soldier, but as a shadow. My job was never to be seen, never to be noticed. I was the man in the background, listening, passing information. Shaping events from behind the curtain."

Rohan crossed his arms. "So why did you leave?"

Bilal's expression turned grim. "I didn't. No one leaves the Order. But I saw something... something I wasn't supposed to. Something bigger than all of us."

I took a step closer. "What did you see?"

For the first time since he started speaking, Bilal hesitated. His hand drifted toward his pocket, but not for a weapon. He pulled out a small, folded piece of paper and handed it to me.

I unfolded it carefully.

At first glance, it looked like an old document, written in a mixture of Latin and Arabic, with a strange symbol at the bottom—an insignia of a coiled serpent encircling a crown.

"This is their original charter," Bilal said. "The foundation of the Sovereign Order, dating back hundreds of years. But look at the last paragraph."

I scanned the text. Then my breath caught in my throat.

"The world is not ruled by nations, but by those who control the unseen."

I swallowed hard.

"They don't care about governments," Bilal said. "They don't care about power in the way most people understand it. Their true goal has always been control of something else entirely."

"What?" Rohan asked, his voice barely above a whisper.

Bilal looked at me, his expression grim.

"History itself."

The Architects of Time

The silence in the tunnel was suffocating. The weight of Bilal's words hung between us like a storm cloud, dark and unrelenting.

I ran my fingers over the aged document, the paper rough and brittle. "History itself," I repeated, the words like acid on my tongue. "What does that mean?"

Bilal's eyes flickered with something I couldn't place—regret, maybe even fear. "The Sovereign Order isn't just manipulating events. They're rewriting them. Altering records. Erasing truths. Crafting a version of history that serves only them."

Rohan let out a sharp breath. "You're saying they've been controlling the past?"

Bilal nodded. "And in doing so, they control the future."

A chill ran through me. I thought back to all the historical events that never quite made sense, the disappearances, the sudden shifts in power, the wars started under mysterious pretenses.

"How?" I asked. "How do they change history itself?"

Bilal glanced at the tunnel's ceiling, as if checking for unseen ears. Then, he lowered his voice.

"Through information. They own the world's largest archives—documents, photographs, first-hand accounts, evidence that proves the truth. And when the truth doesn't serve them, they erase it."

He took the document from my hand and pointed at a single word written in an older dialect. "Custodes."

Rohan frowned. "Guardians?"

Bilal nodded. "The Sovereign Order sees itself as the guardian of human civilization. Not its leaders, not its protectors, but the ones who ensure the right version of history survives."

I swallowed. "Whose version?"

Bilal's jaw clenched. "Theirs."

I exhaled sharply, my mind racing. "So the revolutions, the assassinations, the economic collapses—they weren't just random? The Order orchestrated them?"

Bilal gave a grim nod. "To shape the world in their image. Sometimes they do it through finance, sometimes through war. But when none of that is enough, they do something worse."

A terrible thought began forming in my mind. "They erase people."

"Yes." Bilal's voice was flat. "People who knew too much. People who were threats. They don't just kill them. They erase them from history itself."

Rohan shook his head. "That's impossible. You can't just erase someone."

Bilal turned to him. "Can't you? Think about it—how many great minds, brilliant thinkers, revolutionaries, have vanished? Some were called traitors, some died in 'accidents,' and some… were simply forgotten. The Order makes sure of that. They don't just remove people. They remove every trace of them. Records. Mentions. Stories. Until they never existed in the first place."

I felt cold. This wasn't just control. This was absolute dominion over reality itself.

Rohan ran a hand through his hair, exhaling. "And Mehta? The people chasing us—are they trying to silence us because we found out?"

Bilal's gaze darkened. "No. They're trying to recruit you."

The words hit me like a slap.

"What?"

Bilal took a slow step forward. "Think about it, Detective. They could've killed you a dozen times by now. But they didn't. They tested you. They pushed you to the edge. Because they want to see if you're useful to them."

Rohan's fists clenched. "And what if we refuse?"

Bilal's voice was like ice. "Then you won't exist anymore."

A shudder crawled down my spine. This wasn't just a conspiracy. This was war. And we were already in too deep.

Then, from the darkness ahead, the sound of footsteps.

Bilal stiffened. "They found us." Without another word, we ran deeper into the abyss, toward the unknown.

The Ghost in the Archives

The tunnel seemed to stretch endlessly into darkness. Our footsteps echoed off the damp walls as we ran, the sound of pursuit growing fainter behind us. But we weren't safe—not yet.

Bilal led us through a series of turns, each one more disorienting than the last, until we reached a heavy metal door. It was old, rusted, but still solid. He pulled out a key—one that looked far too modern for such an ancient place—and inserted it into a hidden slot in the stone wall.

With a low mechanical groan, the door slid open.

Inside was something I never expected.

Rows of metal shelves stretched into the distance, lined with files, records, artifacts—history itself. The stale air smelled of aged paper and ink. It was an archive, but not just any archive.

This was where history was rewritten.

Bilal shut the door behind us and turned, his face grim.

"This is one of the Order's hidden vaults," he said. "One of many."

Rohan exhaled sharply. "So this is where they keep the real history?"

"Not just history," Bilal said. "Proof. Documents, original records, things they've erased from the world above. Things they don't want anyone to see."

I stepped forward, running my fingers over a row of old books. Some were in languages I didn't recognize. Some were labeled with names—names of people, events, entire civilizations that shouldn't have been forgotten.

But one file stopped me cold.

It was my name.

My full name, written in bold ink on a folder that looked decades old.

My breath caught in my throat. "What the hell is this?"

Bilal's expression darkened. "I was afraid of this."

I ripped the folder off the shelf and flipped it open. Inside were documents, surveillance photos, transcripts of conversations I didn't even remember having. Dates that didn't make sense. Events that happened before I was even born.

"What is this?" I demanded. "This file is older than me."

Bilal didn't answer right away. He just watched me, his silence heavy.

Then, softly, he said, "Because you weren't supposed to exist."

The words made my skin go cold.

I shook my head. "That's not possible."

Bilal stepped closer. "The Sovereign Order doesn't just erase people. Sometimes… they bring people back. Recreate them. Rewrite them."

I could barely hear my own breathing.

"You're saying…" My voice barely worked. "I'm not real?"

Bilal held my gaze. "You're real. But the life you remember? The past you think is yours? It was designed. Constructed."

I staggered back, my mind spinning. This couldn't be happening. My memories, my past, my entire life—was it all a lie?

I shook my head violently. " I had parents. I had a childhood—"

Bilal reached into the file and pulled out an old photograph. A black-and-white image of a child—a child that looked exactly like me. The date on the bottom? 1924.

I felt like the ground had disappeared beneath me.

"They've been running experiments for decades," Bilal said quietly. "Altering people. Changing their pasts. And you, Detective… you were one of them."

The room felt like it was closing in. The walls, the documents, the weight of a truth too heavy to bear.

I wasn't chasing the Sovereign Order.

I was part of their design all along.

And I never even knew it.

CHAPTER TEN

THE ARCHITECT'S TRUTH

The room felt suffocating. The weight of the files, the history buried within them, the truth Bilal had just revealed—it was too much. My hands trembled as I clutched the photograph, my own face staring back at me from nearly half a century ago.

"This... this is impossible," I whispered. "I was born in 1971. My parents—"

"Were part of the program," Bilal interrupted. "Or at least, that's what you were made to believe."

Rohan stepped forward, his face a storm of disbelief and anger. "This is insane. How the hell could they rewrite someone's entire life?"

Bilal sighed, running a hand through his hair. "The Sovereign Order has had their hands in genetics, memory implantation, historical manipulation—you name it. You were never meant to find this place, but now that you have, there's no going back."

I clenched my fists. "Then start talking. All of it."

Bilal hesitated. Then he turned toward a locked cabinet in the far corner of the archive. With a swift motion, he pulled out another key—sleek, metallic, and unlike anything I'd ever seen. He inserted it into the lock, and the cabinet clicked open. Inside was a single thick dossier, labeled simply: 'The Architect's Project.'

He handed it to me. "If you want the truth, read this."

I flipped it open.

The Architect's Project

The first few pages were dry government reports, filled with cryptic terminology and signatures from people I didn't recognize. But as I flipped further, the words became more sinister.

PROJECT: ARCHITECT
Initiated: 1923
Primary Objective: Preservation and manipulation of historical continuity. Secondary Objective: Controlled adaptation of key individuals for long-term influence.

I kept reading, my pulse hammering.

Subject 04 – Reintegrated in 1971. Memory sequencing completed.

Status: Active.

Designation: Ahaan Mehra.

I nearly dropped the file.

My entire body felt cold.

"They didn't just rewrite my past," I muttered. "They... they built me."

Bilal nodded. "You're what they call a Temporal Adaptation Subject. You, along with a handful of others, were 'reborn' in different eras. You weren't just chosen for this case. You were designed for it."

Rohan looked between us, shaking his head. "Wait, wait. You're saying he's... what? A manufactured person?"

"Not manufactured," Bilal said. "Reconstructed. He existed before. The Order just... rearranged him."

The room spun around me. My memories felt like a fragile house of cards, ready to collapse at any moment.

Then I saw it. A name. At the bottom of the final page, scrawled in thick ink:

The Architect: KABIR MEHRA.

My breath hitched. Mehra. The same last name as mine. Rohan noticed it too. "Is this—?"

"My father," I whispered.

The world tilted. The Sovereign Order hadn't just created me. My own father had been part of it.

And he had erased me.

CHAPTER ELEVEN

THE FORGOTTEN SON

The name burned into my vision like a scar across time.

Kabir Mehra.

Not just some hidden mastermind. Not just another name in the Sovereign Order's twisted records. My father.

The weight of it crushed me, warping my breath into ragged gasps. Memories—no, illusions—flashed through my mind. My childhood. The bedtime stories. The warmth of my mother's voice when she spoke of my father, a man I barely remembered. A man who, as I now realized, had never been truly absent.

He had been orchestrating everything from the shadows.

"Where is he?" I whispered. My fingers clenched around the dossier so hard it crumpled under my grip.

Bilal hesitated. "Gone. Off the grid for years. He vanished after the last stage of the project was completed."

Rohan's voice cut through the heavy silence. "And what was the last stage?"

Bilal turned to me. "You."

The Hidden Program

The room felt colder, as if the truth itself had stolen the warmth from the air.

Bilal pulled out another folder, flipping through pages of encrypted reports and grainy photographs. Then he found what he was looking for. He held up an image.

A lab. Stark white walls, filled with strange pods. Inside one of them, submerged in a translucent liquid—was me.

My breath caught in my throat. "That's not possible."

"You weren't born in 1971," Bilal said quietly. "You were activated."

My pulse thundered in my ears. Rohan was speechless, his hands pressed against his temples as if trying to keep his own mind from shattering.

Bilal continued, his voice eerily calm. "Project Architect was never just about preserving history. It was about controlling it. They needed agents—people who could be inserted at key points in time, with tailored memories and identities, to shape events from within. You were one of their most successful assets."

"But I had a life," I argued. "I remember growing up, going to school, joining the force—"

"They weren't real," Bilal interrupted. "They were built. Fabricated and implanted into your consciousness before you were placed into the world."

I staggered back, gripping the edge of the table for support. "Why me?"

Bilal met my gaze. "Because you were supposed to replace him."

The words hit like a physical blow.

Kabir Mehra hadn't just created me.

He had made me in his own image.

A perfect successor. An heir without history, built to finish what he had started.

Rohan finally spoke, his voice hoarse. "And what exactly did he start?"

Bilal exhaled sharply. "A war. One that hasn't started yet... but is about to."

The War Unseen

Bilal pulled a small, encrypted hard drive from his pocket and plugged it into the console. A series of maps and documents flooded the screen.

Classified communications. Secret meetings. Plans decades in the making.

"The Sovereign Order has been manipulating global events for over a century," Bilal explained. "They don't control governments. They control the decisions that governments make. Wars, economic collapses, assassinations—all carefully calibrated, all part of a greater design."

Rohan let out a shaky laugh. "This is insane."

"It gets worse," Bilal said. "They aren't just planning for the future. They're rewriting the past. And your father… he's the one who started it."

I couldn't breathe. My father hadn't just erased me.

He had built history itself.

And now, he was preparing to erase it again.

Bilal pointed at the screen. "There's a location burned into all the encrypted files. A fail-safe. A place where everything can be reset."

I forced my mind to function, to push past the horror. "Where?"

Bilal locked eyes with me.

"Zurich. The Black Archive."

The words sent a chill down my spine. Because I knew exactly what that was.

A place rumored to contain the Sovereign Order's most dangerous secrets.

A place that wasn't supposed to exist.

A place where, if I didn't stop him, my father would rewrite history once more.

The Successor's Fate

I didn't speak. I couldn't. The words in the file blurred before my eyes as realization struck like lightning. The Sovereign Order had never intended for me to simply uncover the truth. I was meant to replace my father.

"They're not hunting you to kill you," Bilal said grimly. "They're testing you. Every challenge, every moment of survival—it's their way of ensuring you're ready to take Kabir Mehra's place."

My stomach twisted. "And if I refuse?"

Bilal's expression turned solemn. "Then they erase you. For good."

Rohan clenched his fists. "We're not letting that happen. What's their next move?"

Before Bilal could answer, the room shuddered. The distant echo of footsteps. Heavy, synchronized. We'd been found.

Bilal's face hardened. "They're here. We need to leave—NOW."

The vault doors slammed open.

And standing at the threshold, dressed in a black coat, was Kabir Mehra.

My father. Alive.

The Father's Gambit

Kabir stepped forward, his gaze piercing through me like a blade. He looked eerily composed, his expression unreadable.

"Ahaan," he said, his voice smooth but laced with something I couldn't place. "You were never meant to find this place. But now that you have, we have decisions to make."

Rohan reached for an iron rod, but Kabir raised a single hand. "No need for theatrics. If I wanted you dead, you wouldn't have made it this far."

Bilal stepped in front of me, his body tense. "We know everything. The experiments. The manipulation. The truth."

Kabir tilted his head slightly. "And yet, you still don't understand the full picture."

I swallowed hard. "Then enlighten me."

He exhaled slowly, his fingers tracing over one of the classified files. "You think the Sovereign Order is the enemy. That they are villains in some grand scheme. But what if I told you the world only survives because of them?"

Rohan scoffed. "Manipulating history? Controlling people's lives? That's survival?"

Kabir's gaze sharpened. "That's balance. Without intervention, nations crumble. Wars spiral beyond control. The illusion of free will is what keeps people from destroying everything."

My hands clenched into fists. "And you justify all of this by playing god?"

He took a step closer, lowering his voice. "I justify it by preventing collapse. And now, Ahaan, you must decide. You were created for a purpose. To succeed me. The Order is not hunting you; they are waiting for your answer."

A cold silence filled the air.

Bilal shook his head. "Don't listen to him. He's trying to manipulate you just like they always have."

Kabir's eyes never left mine. "Are they? Or have you simply been given a choice you were never prepared for?"

I felt the weight of his words pressing down on me. This wasn't just about survival anymore. This was about something much larger. Something that could shift the balance of power forever.

I had spent my life chasing the truth.

But was I ready to become a part of it?

And if I refused—was I ready to face the consequences?

I took a step back, inhaling sharply. "No. I refuse."

Kabir's expression darkened. "Then you will not survive."

I turned to Bilal and Rohan. "We need to get to Zurich. The Black Archives. If the Sovereign Order wants to control history, then we need to find where it all begins."

Bilal nodded. "Then we have no time to waste."

The room shook with approaching footsteps. The Order's enforcers were coming.

Kabir sighed. "You could have ruled history, Ahaan. Instead, you will be erased by it."

I locked eyes with him one last time. "Then I'll make sure the world knows the truth before they do."

We ran into the tunnels, heading toward our next battle. Zurich. The Black Archives.

The fight wasn't over.

It had only just begun.

CHAPTER TWELVE

THE BLACK ARCHIVES

The flight to Zurich was silent. Each of us sat absorbed in our own thoughts, the weight of our mission pressing down on us. The Sovereign Order had spent centuries burying secrets, erasing people, rewriting history. But if the Black Archives were real, then this was our chance to rip the truth from their hands and expose it to the world.

As the plane descended, the city came into view, its crisp skyline gleaming against the Alps. Zurich—clean, orderly, and beneath its polished surface, a hidden war was being waged.

Bilal turned to me. "If the Order has a fail-safe, this is it. The Black Archives aren't just a library. They're the final record of everything they've ever altered. Every conspiracy, every assassination, every rewritten truth. If we access them, we don't just expose the Order—we burn them to the ground."

Rohan frowned. "And let me guess… they're heavily guarded?"

Bilal smirked. "More than that. They're underground, built beneath an old bank that no longer exists on any official record. The entrance is hidden in the foundation of what was once the Swiss Federal Archives.

The entire place is a fortress. No one gets in without authorization. No one gets out if they're caught."

I clenched my jaw. "Then we'd better make sure we don't get caught."

75

Beneath the Surface

The streets of Zurich were quiet as we made our way to the location. According to Bilal, the entrance was concealed beneath an abandoned churchyard—a relic from a time before the city had been remodeled.

We moved quickly, avoiding surveillance cameras and public spaces. As we reached the desolate site, Bilal led us to an overgrown mausoleum, its stone walls cracked with age. He knelt by a rusted plaque and, after a moment of searching, pressed his fingers against an almost invisible seam.

With a faint hiss, a hidden mechanism clicked into place. The ground beneath us trembled, and then, slowly, a concealed metal door swung open, revealing a staircase leading into the darkness.

"Welcome to history's graveyard," Bilal muttered. "Let's go."

We descended into the underground passage, the air growing colder with every step. The tunnel smelled of damp stone and something else—something mechanical. The deeper we went, the more we could hear the distant hum of unseen machinery.

After what felt like an eternity, the passage opened up into a vast underground chamber.

And that's when we saw it.

Rows upon rows of towering shelves, each one filled with sealed documents, ancient texts, and classified files stretching into the shadows. Glass cases held artifacts that shouldn't exist—fragments of rewritten events, evidence of erased figures, the skeleton of history itself.

The Black Archives weren't just a vault.

They were the Sovereign Order's greatest crime scene.

Ghosts of the Past

"This is it," I whispered, stepping forward. "This is where they keep the truth."

Bilal moved swiftly, scanning the coded labels on the shelves.

"The files we need are deeper inside. They won't make it easy. The most sensitive documents will be locked away. But if we can find the right records, we can prove everything."

Rohan's gaze was sharp. "And then what? We leak them? Send them to the press?"

I nodded. "We end them."

We pressed forward, navigating the endless aisles of forgotten history.

The deeper we went, the more we saw things that should never have been hidden: documents stamped with seals of long-dead nations, photographs of people erased from existence, letters detailing assassinations that had never officially happened.

Then Bilal stopped short. His breath hitched.

"Ahaan…"

He pulled a single file from the shelf, his hands shaking.

It had my name on it.

I took the file from him and opened it. What I saw made my blood turn to ice.

There were two photographs inside.

One was of me—Ahaan Mehra, the man I had always known myself to be.

The second was of someone identical to me. But the photo was dated 1947.

I staggered back. "No. That's impossible."

Bilal's voice was grim. "The Order didn't just rewrite your past. They've been creating you over and over again. Across different eras."

I felt the room spin.

I wasn't just their experiment.

I was their project.

And I had existed far longer than I could remember.

The Assault

A metallic click echoed through the air.

"Step away from the files. Now."

We turned sharply—black-clad enforcers of the Sovereign Order stood at the entrance of the chamber, weapons trained on us. Their faces were concealed behind tactical masks, their posture rigid with lethal intent.

Rohan's hand inched toward Bilal's concealed pistol, but I grabbed his wrist. "Not yet."

Bilal exhaled sharply. "They were waiting for us."

The lead enforcer, his voice distorted through a voice modulator, took a step forward. "Ahaan Mehra. You were never meant to come here."

I clenched my fists. "Yeah, well. I never liked following the rules."

Before he could react, I grabbed a shelf and yanked it down.

The entire row of classified files collapsed, scattering ancient documents everywhere. In the chaos, we moved—Rohan drew a pistol and fired, dropping one enforcer. Bilal dove behind a pillar, pulling out a combat knife.

The chamber erupted into chaos.

A round whizzed past my ear—I ducked and lunged, slamming my elbow into one of the enforcers' throats. He staggered, and I grabbed his rifle, twisting it out of his grip. With a swift motion, I turned it on him and pulled the trigger.

Two down. More coming.

"We need to get to the control room!" Bilal shouted over the gunfire. "If we shut down security, we can get out!"

I nodded and signaled Rohan. "Cover us!"

We sprinted through the aisles, bullets shredding papers and glass as the Order's enforcers closed in. Rohan laid down suppressive fire, keeping them at bay as we crashed through a metal door labeled 'Control Access.'

Inside, a vast server room hummed, screens flickering with encrypted data.

Bilal rushed to a terminal. "Give me thirty seconds!"

We didn't have thirty seconds.

The enforcers were already breaking through.

"Ahaan!" Rohan tossed me a flash grenade. "Buy us time!"

I yanked the pin and threw it toward the entrance. A blinding white flash detonated, followed by deafening silence. The enforcers staggered, momentarily disoriented.

"Got it!" Bilal shouted. "Security is down! Let's move!"

We barreled through an emergency exit, the alarms now silent, the doors unlocked.

But as we emerged into another corridor, a dark figure blocked our path.

Tall. Cloaked. Unmoving.

A voice, smooth and calm, cut through the air.

"Leaving so soon?"

I knew that voice.

Kabir Mehra. My father.

We ran through the emergency exit tunnel, the sounds of distant shouting fading behind us. The moment we surfaced, the cold Zurich air hit my face like a slap.

We had escaped.

But we weren't safe yet.

I turned to Bilal and Rohan. "They'll come after us. We need to go underground."

Bilal nodded. "We'll disappear. But we have what we need. Now, we bring them down."

As the first sirens wailed in the distance, we vanished into the night.

The war wasn't over.

It had just begun.

CHAPTER THIRTEEN

THE HUNT BEGINS

The streets of Zurich blurred past as we sprinted through narrow alleys, weaving between dimly lit buildings and deserted storefronts. The echoes of police sirens bounced off the walls, a constant reminder that we were being hunted—not just by law enforcement, but by the Sovereign Order itself.

Bilal led the way, his instincts razor-sharp as he navigated the labyrinth of backstreets. Rohan was close behind, gripping his pistol, scanning every shadow for threats. My heart pounded against my ribs as I clutched the stolen folder—the key to unraveling everything the Order had spent centuries hiding.

"We need to get off the streets!" Rohan hissed. "They'll have cameras everywhere. If we don't disappear now, we're done."

Bilal didn't slow down. "I have a place. But we need to move fast."

We ducked into a darkened passageway, the air thick with the scent of damp stone. The entrance to an abandoned building loomed ahead, its rusted door slightly ajar. Bilal gestured for us to follow as he slipped inside.

The moment the door shut behind us, we collapsed against the walls, catching our breath. The silence was deafening, broken only by the distant hum of Zurich's city life above us.

I turned to Bilal. "Where are we?"

He pulled out a small flashlight and flicked it on, illuminating a narrow corridor that led deeper underground. "A safe house. One of the last places the Order doesn't control."

Rohan scoffed. "Let's hope you're right."

The Assassin's Warning

We made our way down the corridor, our footsteps muffled by the dust-covered stone.

At the end of the passage, Bilal stopped in front of a heavy steel door. He knocked three times, paused, then struck twice more.

A moment later, the door creaked open. A figure stepped forward, their face hidden beneath the shadow of a hood.

"You're late," the woman said, her voice edging impatiently.

Bilal exhaled sharply. "We ran into complications."

The woman studied us, her gaze lingering on the folder in my hands. "You stole from the Black Archives. Do you have any idea what you've started?"

I straightened. "We know exactly what we've started. The question is—are you going to help us finish it?"

She hesitated, then stepped aside. "Come in. But know this—the Order isn't just hunting you. They've sent someone.

An assassin. A ghost from your past. And he won't stop until you're dead."

A chill ran down my spine. "Who?"

The woman locked eyes with me. "Your father sent him."

Silence fell over the room.

I clenched my fists. "Then we make sure he fails."

A Familiar Shadow

The room was dimly lit, lined with maps, weapons, and scattered intelligence reports. The woman pulled back her hood, revealing sharp green eyes and short dark hair. She exuded an air of controlled danger.

"Name's Esha," she said. "Ex-Order. I walked away from them years ago, but I know how they work. And if your father sent someone after you, it's worse than you think."

I narrowed my eyes. "Who is he?"

Esha hesitated. "His name is Kaveh. They call him 'The Revenant.' He doesn't fail. Ever."

Rohan muttered a curse. "I've heard that name before. Iranian black ops, rumored to have died years ago. But if he's alive… we're dealing with a ghost."

Bilal exhaled. "Ahaan, this isn't just any assassin. Kaveh doesn't hunt. He finishes. The Order only sends him when they want someone erased without a trace."

A cold weight settled in my chest. "Then we don't give him the chance."

Esha nodded. "If you want to survive, we need to leave this safe house. He'll find it soon. We need to move—now."

A sudden thud from above made us freeze.

Rohan drew his gun. "Too late. He's here."

The lights flickered. A single red laser beam traced across the room before vanishing into the darkness.

Then, a voice. Calm. Controlled. Deadly.

"You should have run faster." The door exploded inward.

The Revenant Strikes

The blast sent shards of wood and metal flying through the air. I barely had time to react before a shadow darted through the dust, moving impossibly fast.

Kaveh.

I ducked as a blade whistled past my ear, embedding itself into the concrete wall. Rohan fired three quick shots, but Kaveh was already gone, slipping into the darkness like a phantom.

"Scatter!" Esha shouted.

We split apart as Kaveh reappeared, his movements precise, methodical. He didn't rush—he didn't need to. He was a predator who had already cornered his prey.

Bilal lunged at him, knife in hand, but Kaveh caught his wrist and twisted. The sickening sound of bone snapping filled the room as Bilal collapsed with a pained scream.

"Bilal!" I surged forward, swinging a broken chair leg at Kaveh's head. He dodged effortlessly, but it gave Esha enough time to fire her sidearm.

The bullet grazed his shoulder.

For the first time, Kaveh faltered.

I pressed the advantage, tackling him into a table. We crashed to the ground, grappling for control. His strength was inhuman—each movement deliberate, each strike meant to kill.

His hand clamped around my throat, squeezing hard.

Black spots filled my vision. My fingers scrabbled against his wrist, desperate for air.

Then a gunshot. Rohan's bullet tore through Kaveh's side.

The assassin staggered, his grip loosening just enough for me to break free. I didn't hesitate. I grabbed a shattered piece of metal and drove it into his shoulder.

Kaveh fell back, his cold eyes locking onto mine.

Even injured, he was still dangerous.

But he wasn't invincible.

Esha grabbed Bilal, hauling him up. "We need to go! Now!"

I backed toward the exit, keeping my gaze on Kaveh. He wasn't following—not yet. He was studying us.

"This isn't over," he said, his voice as calm as ever. "I will find you again. And next time, you won't be so lucky."

I clenched my jaw. "Next time, I'll be ready."

We burst through the back door into the night, disappearing into the city streets.

We had survived.

But Kaveh was still out there.

And he wasn't done hunting us yet.

CHAPTER FOURTEEN

NO SAFE HAVEN

The cold Zurich air bit into my skin as we ran, our breaths ragged and uneven. We had escaped Kaveh—for now. But I knew better than to think he wouldn't come after us again.

Bilal groaned, his arm hanging limp at his side, pain written all over his face. His wrist was shattered, and we didn't have the luxury of medical attention. We needed to disappear. Fast.

Esha led us through the darkened streets, avoiding cameras, moving with precision. "There's an old network of tunnels beneath the city," she said. "If we get there, we can disappear. But we need to hurry."

I nodded, gripping the stolen folder tighter. This wasn't just about survival anymore. This was about ending the Sovereign Order.

The Underground Refuge

Esha guided us through a maze of abandoned buildings until we reached a hidden entrance behind a derelict church. She yanked open a rusted grate, revealing a passage descending into darkness.

"Move. Quickly," she urged.

One by one, we climbed down. The tunnels smelled of damp earth and rusted iron. The flickering lights overhead barely illuminated the narrow passage.

Bilal leaned against the wall, wincing. Rohan stood guard at the entrance, his gun ready.

"We can't stay here long," Rohan said. "Kaveh will track us soon."

Esha pulled out a folded map, laying it on the stone floor. "There's a way out through the old industrial sector. If we reach the rail yard, I have someone waiting to get us out of Switzerland. But…"

She hesitated.

I narrowed my eyes. "But what?"

She exhaled. "There's a traitor among us. That's how Kaveh found us so quickly. And if we don't figure out who it is… we're dead."

Silence fell over the group.

Rohan's grip on his gun tightened. "You better start explaining."

Betrayal in the Dark

Esha's eyes darted between us, calculating. "Think about it. The Order shouldn't have known our exact location. Someone tipped them off. And it had to be one of us."

Bilal groaned, shaking his head. "That's ridiculous. We've been fighting together since this began. If one of us were working with the Order, why would they risk their own life?"

Esha shrugged. "Loyalty is a funny thing. Maybe they had no choice. Maybe they were bought. Either way, Kaveh's precision was no coincidence."

I clenched my fists. "We don't have time for paranoia. We need to move."

But the seed of doubt had already been planted.

Was it possible? Had someone betrayed us?

As we packed up, I watched them—Bilal clutching his wounded arm, Rohan scanning the tunnels for threats, Esha ready to run at a moment's notice.

Someone in this group had led Kaveh to us.

I just didn't know who.

Nowhere Left to Run

The tunnels led us to an underground drainage system. It was our only way to the industrial sector, but as we stepped inside, the walls trembled.

A distant boom echoed through the tunnels.

Esha cursed. "They found us! Move!"

We ran. Hard.

Behind us, the tunnels collapsed as explosives detonated, cutting off our exit. Shadows moved in the distance—the Order's enforcers pouring into the tunnels.

A gunshot rang out.

I dove for cover as bullets ricocheted off the walls. Rohan returned fire, dropping one of the attackers.

"Keep moving!" Bilal yelled, his voice strained from pain.

We sprinted toward the exit, our only hope of escape. But just as we reached the final tunnel—

Kaveh stepped into the light.

Gun raised.

Smirking.

"Going somewhere?"

THE REVENANT'S WRATH

Kaveh's presence filled the tunnel with a suffocating sense of inevitability. His dark eyes glowed under the dim emergency lights, his grip on the silenced pistol steady. There was no hesitation in his stance—only the certainty of a man who had never failed a mission.

"Drop your weapons," he ordered, his voice eerily calm. "You've run long enough."

Rohan didn't waste time. He fired. The gunshot echoed through the narrow passage, but Kaveh was already moving. He twisted his body, the bullet missing him by mere inches, and returned fire in a single, controlled motion. The shot struck Rohan's shoulder, spinning him backward.

Bilal lunged forward despite his injuries, attempting to tackle Kaveh, but the assassin sidestepped effortlessly. One swift movement. One precise strike. Bilal crumpled to the ground, gasping for breath, clutching his ribs in agony.

"You're making this too easy," Kaveh said, barely winded. "Your father trained me well, Ahaan. Better than you."

I clenched my jaw. "Then let's see if I can surprise you."

I grabbed a loose metal pipe from the debris and swung it toward Kaveh's head. He ducked, barely avoiding the strike, and countered with a knife aimed for my ribs. I twisted away at the last second, the blade slicing fabric instead of flesh.

Esha moved in from behind, pulling out a hidden blade. Kaveh sensed it—too late. She plunged the knife into his side, a rare look of shock flashing across his face as blood stained his coat.

But he didn't fall. He smiled.

"Not bad," he admitted, before slamming his elbow into her temple.

Esha hit the ground hard, momentarily stunned. I took the opening, driving my knee into his wounded side, forcing him back.

Kaveh staggered, eyes darkening. "You think you've won? You don't even know what you've stolen."

I gritted my teeth. "Then why don't you enlighten me?"

He wiped the blood from his lips, exhaling slowly. "That folder isn't just a record of the Order's history. It's their contingency plan. If you think they'll let you live after what you've taken, you're already dead."

A sinking feeling crept into my gut.

Kaveh's earpiece crackled to life. A voice on the other end spoke in a language I didn't recognize, but I understood its meaning all too well.

Backup was coming. We were out of time.

Esha pushed herself up, eyes still hazy. "We need to go. Now."

I grabbed Bilal, pulling him onto his feet. Rohan clutched his wounded shoulder, grimacing. We turned to escape—

Kaveh chuckled, barely standing. "Run while you can. I'll find you again. I always do."

I met his gaze one last time. "Next time, I'll be the one hunting you."

We disappeared into the tunnels as the Sovereign Order closed in.

95

CHAPTER SIXTEEN

THE CONTINGENCY PLAN

The tunnels stretched on endlessly, damp and suffocating, but we kept moving.

Every step echoed against the walls, our breath labored from exhaustion and the adrenaline of our narrow escape.

Kaveh was wounded, but he wouldn't stay down for long. And if backup was coming, we had minutes—maybe seconds—before the Sovereign Order closed in on us.

Esha led us deeper underground until we reached a rusted service hatch. With a swift kick, she forced it open, revealing a maintenance tunnel that ran beneath the Zurich rail yards. We climbed through, emerging into a dark storage room stacked with crates and old machinery.

Bilal slumped against a crate, his face pale. "We need to stop. Just for a moment."

Rohan winced as he tore a piece of fabric from his shirt, pressing it against his bleeding shoulder. "We don't have a moment. If Kaveh's still alive, he'll track us. And if his men find us first—"

"Then we don't let them," I interrupted, catching my breath. "We need to figure out what's in that folder. If Kaveh was willing to die for it, then it's more than just a list of names. It's the Order's insurance policy."

Esha pulled out a small flashlight, flipping through the pages of the stolen documents. Her eyes narrowed as she skimmed the contents. "It's worse than we thought. This isn't just about the past. It's about what's coming next."

I stepped closer. "What do you mean?"

She turned the file around, pointing at a series of encrypted codes and dates. "These are coordinated events. Planned disasters, political assassinations, economic crashes—all orchestrated by the Order to maintain their control. This isn't history. This is the future."

Bilal exhaled sharply. "You're saying the Sovereign Order isn't just covering their tracks? They're planning new ones?"

Esha nodded grimly. "And one of these events is set to happen in less than a week."

The Countdown

The realization hit like a sledgehammer. We weren't just running for our lives. We were racing against time. The document laid out a list of global power plays—ones that would cement the Order's influence for decades to come.

Rohan pointed to one of the codenames listed under the upcoming events. "Project Nightfall. What the hell is that?"

Esha flipped through more pages, her expression darkening. "It's an assassination plan. A high-profile political figure. If they succeed, it'll trigger a war."

I clenched my fists. "Who's the target?"

She hesitated. "The Prime Minister of the United Kingdom. He's set to attend a private summit in Geneva in four days."

Silence filled the room.

Bilal shook his head. "If they pull this off, they won't just control history. They'll dictate the future."

I stood up, feeling the weight of responsibility settle over me like a lead blanket. "Then we stop it. We go to Geneva. We stop Nightfall."

Esha looked at me like I'd lost my mind. "We barely survived Kaveh. Now you want to take on an entire shadow government?"

I met her gaze. "If we don't, millions will suffer. The Order wins. And everything we've done—everyone we've lost—will mean nothing."

Rohan exhaled, checking his gun. "Then we better find a way into that summit."

A Dangerous Alliance

Getting into a high-security political summit wasn't going to be easy. We needed fake credentials, a solid plan, and most importantly—information from someone on the inside.

Bilal groaned as he shifted. "I might know a guy. He used to run black-market IDs for European diplomats. If he's still in business, he can get us in."

Esha crossed her arms. "And where do we find this miracle worker?"

Bilal smirked. "Paris."

I sighed. "Of course it's Paris."

The plan was taking shape. We had our target, we had a way in, but one question remained—

Who was the traitor?

Kaveh had found us too easily. Someone in our group had given us up. And if they did it once, they'd do it again.

I scanned my team. Bilal was injured but loyal. Rohan had saved my life more than once. Esha was ruthless but had risked herself to fight Kaveh. One of them was lying. And I needed to find out who before we reached Paris.

Because if I didn't, we wouldn't make it to Geneva alive.

The First Move

We left Zurich before sunrise, slipping onto a cargo train heading for France. The ride was rough, the compartments freezing, but it kept us hidden.

Rohan sat across from me, cleaning his pistol. "If this contact of Bilal's sells us out, we're dead."

Bilal scowled. "He won't. He owes me."

Esha was scanning the stolen documents again, her eyes darting between pages. "We need to assume the Order already knows we have these files. They won't let us get to Geneva."

I leaned against the metal wall. "Then we hit first. No more running. We turn the hunt back on them."

Rohan raised an eyebrow. "And how do we do that?"

I smirked. "We bait the trap."

Bilal groaned. "I don't like where this is going."

I held up one of the encrypted pages. "This file says Nightfall has multiple operatives. If we can intercept one of them, we can extract intel. And I think I know where they'll be."

Esha leaned forward. "Where?"

"Paris," I said. "The same place we're headed."

The plan was set. We would find the Order's operative in Paris, uncover their plan, and stop Nightfall before it began.

But as the train rattled forward, I couldn't shake the feeling that something was about to go terribly wrong.

Someone in our group was working against us.

And soon, I'd have to face them.

CHAPTER SEVENTEEN

INTO THE LION'S DEN

The train rattled into Paris just before dawn, its steel wheels screeching against the tracks as we pulled into an industrial freight yard on the outskirts of the city. We had taken every precaution—no tickets, no passports, nothing that could trace us back to Zurich. But I knew that wouldn't be enough. The Sovereign Order had eyes everywhere.

The city was waking up. Neon signs flickered to life, early commuters hurried through the streets, and somewhere in the heart of it all, an Order operative was preparing for Project Nightfall.

I turned to my team as we slipped off the train, avoiding security patrols. "We need to split up. Less of a target that way. Bilal, find your contact. Get us those IDs. Esha, I want surveillance on the summit location—routes, security, potential weak points. Rohan, you're with me. We find the operative and figure out who the hell we're dealing with."

Bilal nodded, adjusting his sling. "I'll meet you at the safehouse in Montmartre. Midnight."

Esha pulled her hood up. "If I'm not there by then, assume I'm compromised."

I exhaled, gripping the folder hidden beneath my jacket. "Let's get to work."

The Hunt Once Again

Rohan and I moved fast through the city streets, blending with the morning crowds. I had studied the stolen documents on the train, memorizing the encrypted coordinates tied to Nightfall's operatives. One location stood out—a luxury hotel in the 8th arrondissement.

As we approached the building, Rohan muttered, "This place screams money. The Order definitely has someone inside."

We slipped into the lobby, pretending to be weary travelers. Chandeliers sparkled overhead, casting golden light over the marble floors. We weren't alone.

I spotted him near the bar—our target.

A man in a sharp suit, sipping an espresso, casually checking his watch. He had the look of someone used to power, someone who didn't need to hide. That made him dangerous.

Rohan leaned in. "What's the play?"

I smirked. "We make an introduction."

A Dance with the Devil

I approached the man and slid into the seat across from him. He barely looked up from his cup.

"You're not the usual company I keep," he said, swirling his espresso. "But you knew I'd be here. That means you've been reading stolen files."

I forced a smile. "And you knew we'd come for you. That means you have something worth protecting."

He finally looked up, his eyes like polished obsidian. "They call me Adrien. And you're in way over your head."

I leaned forward. "Tell me about Nightfall."

Adrien chuckled. "You don't stop a storm by catching raindrops. Nightfall is inevitable."

Rohan's hand twitched near his gun. "Unless we make it personal."

Adrien smirked. "You think you can threaten me? You have no idea what you're really up against. The Order isn't just powerful—it's everywhere. And you, Ahaan Mehra, are already dead."

The words sent a chill down my spine. He knew my name.

Before I could react, Adrien flipped the espresso cup toward me. Boiling liquid splashed across my hand as he reached for a hidden knife.

The fight was on.

A Deadly Encounter

Rohan moved first. A gunshot shattered the lobby's calm. Adrien twisted away at the last second, the bullet embedding into the bar counter. Patrons screamed and scattered.

I lunged forward, grabbing Adrien's wrist before his blade could find my throat. He was fast. Too fast. He slammed his elbow into my ribs, knocking the air from my lungs.

"You can't stop what's coming," he growled. "Nightfall has already begun."

I headbutted him. Hard.

Adrien stumbled, blood dripping from his nose, but he was already reaching for a pistol inside his jacket.

Rohan tackled him before he could fire. The two crashed to the ground, grappling for control. Adrien twisted, smashing a knee into Rohan's gut. He was going to kill him.

I didn't think. I acted.

I grabbed a broken champagne bottle from the floor and drove it into Adrien's shoulder.

He let out a strangled gasp, his grip on the gun loosening. Rohan wrenched the weapon away and pressed it against Adrien's temple.

"Talk," Rohan snarled. "Or I paint this floor red."

Adrien coughed, chuckling even as blood soaked his expensive suit. "It's too late. Your traitor already gave you up."

Everything froze. My blood turned to ice.

"What did you say?" I demanded.

Adrien smirked, his breath ragged. "You think I found you on my own? Someone close to you made a deal. And now… you're walking into a trap."

Rohan exchanged a glance with me. The traitor.

"Who?" I pressed the gun harder against his chest. "Who sold us out?"

Adrien's eyes flickered with amusement. "Find out for yourself."

Then, he bit down hard on something inside his mouth.

A cyanide capsule.

Within seconds, he was dead.

Nowhere to Hide

We left the hotel through the service exit, hearts pounding. The Order had planned for this. We weren't hunting them—they were hunting us.

We had one option left: find the traitor before they finished the job.

By midnight, we were back at the safehouse in Montmartre. The room was dark, the air thick with tension.

Esha was already there, her arms crossed. Bilal sat on the couch, his expression unreadable.

I placed my gun on the table. "One of us betrayed the team. Adrien confirmed it before he died."

Silence.

Bilal's jaw tightened. "You really think it's one of us? We've been through hell together."

"Someone gave the Order our movements. Someone led Kaveh to us. And now they're setting up the final play in Geneva."

Esha's eyes darkened. "We don't have time for suspicion. We need to move."

I scanned the faces in front of me. One of them was lying.

The tension was suffocating. But before I could press further, the safehouse windows shattered.

A red laser dot appeared on Rohan's chest.

"Snipers! Get down!"

Gunfire erupted. The Order had found us.

We weren't safe anymore. We were trapped.

No Room for Doubt

Gunfire ripped through the walls, sending shards of wood and plaster raining down on us. The safehouse was compromised, and we were sitting ducks.

"Move!" I shouted, diving for cover as another round of bullets shattered the lamp above us. Rohan flipped the table, using it as a makeshift barricade, while Bilal dragged his injured body toward the hallway.

Esha fired back through the broken window. "They're on the rooftops! Sniper teams! We need an exit, now!"

I scanned the room. One way out. The back door leading to the alley.

"Cover me!" I sprinted for the hallway, kicking the door open. Bad idea. The moment I stepped through, I came face to face with an Order enforcer. He was already pulling the trigger.

I twisted at the last second. The bullet grazed my arm, pain exploding through my shoulder. But I didn't stop. I grabbed the enforcer's wrist, twisted it, and forced the gun toward the ceiling. One punch to the throat—he staggered. Rohan rushed in behind me, finishing him with a clean shot.

"Go!" Rohan yelled.

We pushed into the alley, the night air thick with smoke. Sirens wailed in the distance—Paris police were closing in.

"Split up," Esha ordered. "Regroup at the fallback point."

"And if we don't make it?" Bilal asked.

"Then you better make it."

With that, we vanished into the streets of Montmartre, the Sovereign Order hunting us like prey.

The Streets of Montmartre

I ran through the narrow alleyways, my heart pounding. I could hear footsteps behind me—fast, controlled, professional. The Order's men were on my trail.

Think, Ahaan.

Montmartre was a maze. I ducked through an old market street, weaving through street vendors packing up for the night. A fruit cart toppled behind me as a bullet shattered its wooden frame. Close. Too close.

A turn. Another alley. Dead end.

"Shit."

The enforcer chasing me slowed, stepping into the dim light of the alley. He smirked. He thought he had me.

I raised my hands. "Alright, let's talk about this."

The enforcer leveled his pistol at me. "No talking. Just dying."

I sighed. "You guys really need new dialogue."

Then I kicked the loose drainpipe beside me. It snapped free, crashing onto him. In the half-second of confusion, I lunged. One punch. A knee to the gut. I grabbed his wrist, twisted—snap. His gun hit the ground.

"Nighty night," I muttered, slamming his head against the wall.

I picked up the gun and took off running again. I had to find the others.

The Betrayal Unmasked

I reached the fallback point—a run-down bookstore tucked away in an abandoned part of the district. Rohan and Esha were already there, catching their breath. Bilal was missing.

"Where's Bilal?" I asked.

Esha didn't answer right away. Rohan rubbed his shoulder, wincing. "That's what we need to talk about."

Something in his tone set me on edge. "What happened?"

Esha looked at me. "Bilal isn't coming. He sold us out."

I froze. The words didn't make sense.

"No. That's not possible. He—"

Rohan cut me off. "Adrien was right. The traitor was with us the whole time. And now? He's gone."

My hands clenched into fists. "You're saying Bilal was working for the Order? He's the reason Kaveh found us?"

Esha exhaled, pushing a torn piece of paper across the table. It was from Bilal's pocket—a coded message.

It read: "Mission complete. Rendezvous at final location."

Rohan slammed his fist against the wall. "He led them straight to us. And now he's gone to Geneva."

I swallowed the anger bubbling inside me. Bilal had fought beside us. Bled with us. And now he was the enemy?

"We go after him," I said, my voice cold. "No more running. No more hiding. We end this."

Esha nodded. "Then it's time for Geneva."

113

A Reckoning in Geneva

We boarded the earliest train out of Paris, slipping through security with forged passports. The ride was tense, silent. Nobody spoke about Bilal.

But I knew we were all thinking the same thing.

This wasn't just a mission anymore. It was personal.

Geneva loomed ahead, its skyline shimmering under the morning sun. The summit was only two days away.

And somewhere in the city, Bilal was waiting.

I leaned back in my seat, gripping my gun. If Bilal had made his choice, then so had I.

I was going to find him.

And this time…

There would be no escape.

CHAPTER NINETEEN

THE FINAL HUNT

The air in Geneva was crisp, but the weight on my chest made it hard to breathe.

This city, with its perfect skyline and pristine streets, was about to become a battlefield. Somewhere in these avenues, behind the expensive suits and diplomatic handshakes, Bilal was waiting.

Two days. That's all we had before the summit began. Two days to stop Project Nightfall, to stop the Sovereign Order from unleashing whatever chaos they had planned. Two days to find Bilal and make him answer for his betrayal.

Rohan adjusted his coat, shifting his injured shoulder uncomfortably. "So, where do we start?"

Esha pulled out a burner phone, already dialing a number. "We need eyes on the ground. I have a contact here. Someone who knows how the Order moves."

"And can we trust this person?" I asked.

Esha smirked. "No. But they hate the Order more than they hate me. That's good enough."

A Game of Ghosts

We met Esha's contact in a dimly lit café near the United Nations headquarters. The man—gray-haired, sharp-eyed, and dressed like a forgotten Cold War spy—stirred his tea as if he had all the time in the world.

"Ahaan Mehra," he said without looking up. "You've caused quite a mess."

I raised an eyebrow. "You know me?"

"I make it my business to know dead men walking."

Rohan sighed. "Great. Another optimist."

The man chuckled, finally meeting my gaze. "Name's Gregor. Former intelligence, long since retired. I don't take sides. But I do sell information. And right now, you need it."

I slid a thick envelope across the table—payment, untraceable. "We need Bilal's location. And we need it now."

Gregor leaned back, flipping through a small notebook. "Your friend is playing a dangerous game. He's holed up in a secure apartment near the lakeside. But that's not the interesting part."

Esha crossed her arms. "Enlighten us."

Gregor smirked. "He's not alone. He's meeting with an Order high-rank. Someone big. And if you're planning to crash the party... you're going to need a miracle."

I cracked my knuckles. "Good thing we specialize in miracles."

The Price of Betrayal

We reached the apartment just before sunset. A luxury penthouse, heavily guarded. Bilal had moved up in the world.

"How do you want to do this?" Rohan whispered. "Guns blazing? Or something subtle?"

Esha smirked. "We could pretend to be room service."

I shot her a look. "How about something that doesn't get us killed in the first five minutes?"

We positioned ourselves on a rooftop across the street. Through binoculars, I saw him—Bilal, standing near the window, talking to someone.

I clenched my fists. He looked calm. Unbothered. Like he hadn't just destroyed everything we built.

Then I saw the man he was meeting.

Kaveh.

My stomach turned to ice.

"Tell me I'm hallucinating," Rohan muttered.

"Nope," Esha said. "That's him. The Revenant himself. Alive and well."

Kaveh handed Bilal a file. They were planning something big.

I exhaled slowly. "We move tonight. We take Bilal. And we end this."

The Storm Breaks

Nightfall. We moved like shadows, slipping past security and up the stairwell. The apartment was on the 21st floor.

"This is too easy," Rohan muttered.

As if on cue, the moment we reached the 20th floor, alarms blared.

"Well, shit," Esha said. "Looks like they were expecting us."

The elevator doors burst open—gunmen.

I dove for cover as bullets shredded the walls. Rohan returned fire, dropping two enforcers, while Esha took down a third with a knife to the throat.

"Move!" I shouted. We sprinted up the last flight of stairs, kicking open the penthouse door.

Bilal stood in the center of the room, waiting.

"I was wondering when you'd come, Ahaan," he said calmly.

I raised my gun. "Give me one reason not to put a bullet in you."

He sighed, shaking his head. "Because you need me. And because if you kill me... you'll never stop Nightfall."

Kaveh stepped forward from the shadows, smirking. "Welcome to the endgame."

The Truth We Never Saw

The standoff was electric. Guns drawn. Tension thick enough to choke on.

"So, what's the plan, Bilal?" I asked. "Sell us out again? Or do you just enjoy being a snake?"

Bilal's expression hardened. "You still don't get it, do you? The Order isn't just about power. It's about control. And the only way to break it... is from the inside."

Esha scoffed. "Oh, you're a double agent now? How convenient."

Bilal glared at her. "If you'd stop thinking with your gun for five seconds, you'd realize I'm trying to help you."

Kaveh chuckled. "And they say I'm the manipulator."

Bilal turned to me. "Ahaan, I didn't betray you. I made a choice. The only choice that gives us a real chance."

"By handing us over?"

Bilal shook his head. "By giving you a way into the summit. The Order thinks I'm loyal. That means I have access. You want to stop Nightfall? Then you need me alive."

Silence.

Esha looked at me. "Tell me you're not seriously considering this."

I studied Bilal. Everything told me not to trust him. But...

"We use him," I said finally. "If he's lying, we put a bullet in his head."

Bilal nodded. "Fair enough."

Kaveh smirked. "Oh, this is going to be fun."

The Last Move

We left the penthouse with a plan—crash the summit, expose the Order, and end this once and for all.

But as we walked into the night, I couldn't shake the feeling this wasn't over.

Bilal had chosen his side.

Now, I had to decide if I believed him.

And if I didn't…

I'd be the one to pull the trigger.

CHAPTER TWENTY

A Step into the Fire

The summit was set to begin in less than twenty-four hours, and we were about to walk straight into the belly of the beast. Geneva's city center was a fortress crawling with legitimate and hidden security. The Sovereign Order wasn't just preparing for a political event; they were staging a global power shift.

The plan was simple: infiltrate the summit, locate the Order's control center, expose Project Nightfall, and, if necessary, burn it all to the ground.

The only problem? We had to trust Bilal to get us inside.

I adjusted the collar of my borrowed tuxedo, feeling like a fraud in the sea of politicians and dignitaries around me. The lavish ballroom shimmered with chandeliers, and waiters moved seamlessly between guests, serving drinks to men and women who could make—or break—countries with a signature.

Esha, dressed in an emerald evening gown, leaned against the bar and muttered into her comm. "This is the worst plan we've ever had."

Rohan, in a crisp black suit, smirked. "That's because you weren't around for the train incident."

"What train incident?"

"Exactly."

Bilal, looking far too comfortable in his tailored suit, strode through the room like he belonged there. And maybe he did. He had always been a chameleon—blending in, making people believe whatever they needed to.

"Eyes up," he murmured. "Security's tight, but I have clearance. Play your roles, and we'll get through."

I gritted my teeth. "If you screw us over—"

"You'll kill me. Yes, yes. We've covered that. Now smile, Ahaan. You look like you just swallowed a lemon."

I forced a grin, resisting the urge to punch him. It was going to be a long night.

The Backdoor to Chaos

Bilal led us through a side corridor, flashing his credentials at a guard who barely glanced at them. We passed through a secondary security checkpoint, where a biometric scanner verified his identity. A steel door hissed open.

We stepped inside what looked like a high-tech war room. Screens lined the walls, displaying encrypted feeds, live satellite surveillance, and an active countdown.

Esha nudged me. "Tell me that's not what I think it is."

I swallowed hard. 00:12:45.

Rohan swore under his breath. "Twelve minutes? We thought we had a day!"

Bilal's face hardened. "They moved up the timeline. We stop this now, or we don't stop it at all."

I turned to Esha. "Can you disable the system?"

She cracked her knuckles. "Please. I've hacked into bank vaults harder than this."

As Esha went to work, Bilal scanned the screens. "They have a failsafe. If we don't shut it down in time, they'll trigger an emergency lockdown."

"And then what?" Rohan asked.

Bilal met my gaze. "Then we fight our way out."

The Art of Improvising

The moment Esha accessed the system, alarms blared.

"You had one job," I muttered.

"Oh, I'm sorry, I thought you wanted me to disable the mass-murder countdown!" Esha snapped. "Maybe next time, I'll just let the world burn."

"Less arguing, more escaping!" Rohan shouted, pulling out his gun as guards stormed in.

Gunfire erupted.

Bilal tackled a guard, wrenching the rifle from his hands. I swung a chair at another, sending him sprawling. Esha, still typing frantically, yelled, "I need two more minutes!"

"We don't have two minutes!" I fired at a camera, taking out their surveillance.

Bilal tossed a smoke grenade. "Then stall them!"

The room filled with thick, white smoke. Coughing, I grabbed Esha and pulled her toward the exit. "Tell me you got it!"

She grinned, holding up a flash drive. "I got it."

"Great. Now let's run!"

The Last Stand

We barreled through the corridors as sirens wailed across the building. Kaveh was waiting for us.

He stood at the final exit, a knife twirling in his hand, a gun holstered at his hip. "Going somewhere?"

Bilal exhaled. "You really need a new hobby."

Kaveh smirked. "And you need new friends."

Then he lunged.

I barely dodged as the knife whizzed past my face. I countered with a punch, but Kaveh was already twisting, slamming an elbow into my ribs. Pain exploded through my side.

"You always were predictable," he said, grabbing my wrist and twisting it back. "And too sentimental. That's why you'll lose."

I gritted my teeth. "Funny. I was thinking the same thing about you."

Esha aimed her gun at him. "Back off, or I ventilate you."

Kaveh's smirk didn't waver. "Go ahead. Waste your bullets."

Rohan stepped forward. "Or we can do this the easy way."

"There is no easy way," Kaveh whispered, pressing a button on his wristwatch. The building locks engaged.

Bilal's eyes widened. "He's sealing the exits!"

Kaveh backed toward the control panel. "You didn't think I'd let you walk out of here, did you?"

I threw myself at him before he could hit another button. We crashed through the glass partition, tumbling into the emergency stairwell.

I landed first—badly. Kaveh recovered faster, looming over me.

"Any last words?" he asked.

I grinned. "Yeah. You should really watch your step."

Then I kicked him. Hard.

Kaveh's balance faltered. He slipped.

For the first time, his expression changed—shock.

Then he plummeted down the stairwell.

Esha peered over the railing. "So... that's it? He's just... gone?"

Bilal shook his head. "Trust me. People like him don't die that easily."

Rohan reloaded his gun. "Then let's make sure we're not here when he wakes up."

We emerged into the Geneva night, battered but victorious. The flash drive held everything—the Order's plans, its operatives, its weaknesses.

Bilal turned to me. "Now what?"

I exhaled. Now we end them.

Rohan grinned. "Well, if we survive, drinks are on you."

Esha smirked. "Assuming we don't get arrested first."

Sirens blared in the distance. No time to celebrate.

We disappeared into the city.

The war wasn't over. But tonight... we had won.

CHAPTER TWENTY-ONE

THE SOVEREIGN ORDER STRIKES BACK

The streets of Geneva blurred past as we moved like ghosts, avoiding cameras and checkpoints. The flash drive in my pocket felt heavier than anything I'd ever carried. We had the Order's secrets. But they weren't going to let us walk away.

Bilal led the way through an underground passage beneath an abandoned train station. Rohan, still catching his breath, muttered, "Can we just have one victory where we don't have to immediately run for our lives? Just one? Is that too much to ask?"

Esha smirked. "Welcome to our world. You get one win, and then life slaps you in the face."

"If life slaps me one more time, I swear I'm slapping it back."

Bilal stopped at a rusted door and checked his watch. "We've got a window before the Order locks down the city. If we make it to the airstrip, we're clear."

I nodded. "Then let's move."

The moment we stepped into the open, I knew something was wrong. The streets were too quiet. No police sirens. No traffic. Too perfect.

Esha swore. "It's a trap."

The rooftops erupted in gunfire. Snipers.

"COVER!" I yelled, diving behind an overturned car. Bullets tore through the concrete, sending sparks flying. Rohan fired back, taking down one of the shooters.

Bilal crawled to my side. "We need an exit—NOW!"

I scanned the street. "That alley! We move on three!"

Esha tossed a smoke grenade, covering our path. "Three!" she shouted.

We sprinted into the alley, dodging bullets, the world exploding around us. The Order wasn't playing games anymore. They wanted us erased.

A black SUV screeched into the alley, cutting off our escape. The doors flew open. Armed men poured out.

Rohan panted. "Oh great. They sent the welcoming committee."

I tightened my grip on my gun. "Then let's welcome them properly."

Fighting Fire with Fire

They moved fast. We moved faster.

Bilal tackled the first enforcer, yanking his gun free and using it against him. Esha ducked a swing from another and snapped his arm like a twig.

A gun cocked behind me. Too late.

A shot rang out. But I wasn't hit.

Bilal stood over the fallen enforcer, his gun smoking. He looked at me. "You're welcome."

I exhaled. "Remind me to not kill you later."

We ran for the bridge. If we could cross it, we'd reach the safe zone.

"Go!" I shouted, but the moment we reached the halfway point, two black helicopters roared overhead.

"Oh, come on!" Rohan groaned. "Since when do cults get helicopters?!"

The bridge exploded in front of us, cutting off our escape. We skidded to a halt as Kaveh stepped out of the smoke.

Alive. Unharmed. And grinning.

"Going somewhere?" he asked.

Esha glared. "I hate this guy. I really do."

Kaveh adjusted his cuffs. "You should've stayed in the shadows. But you just couldn't resist poking the beast. And now..." He gestured around him. The Order had us surrounded.

I clenched my fists. "Then let's poke it some more."

The Last Gamble

There was no running now. No tricks left.

Just us versus them.

Kaveh smiled. "Any last words?"

Rohan tilted his head. "Yeah. Have you ever considered therapy? You seem very… stabby."

Before Kaveh could reply, Esha detonated the explosives we'd planted on the bridge.

The shockwave threw everyone off balance. I grabbed Bilal and jumped.

We hit the water below as debris rained around us. Cold. Sharp. Merciless.

The last thing I saw before sinking into darkness was Kaveh watching us fall.

And smiling.

I gasped awake, coughing up water. We'd survived. Barely.

Rohan groaned. "Please tell me I'm dead."

Bilal smirked. "Not yet. But if we don't move, we will be."

Esha pulled herself onto the riverbank. "Kaveh let us escape."

I clenched my jaw. "No. He's playing a longer game. He's not done with us yet."

Bilal sat up. "Then what do we do?"

I looked at the flash drive. "We finish this. We take the fight to them. One last time."

The war wasn't over. But we were done running.

CHAPTER TWENTY-TWO

THE FINAL BATTLE BEGINS

The cold night air clung to us as we huddled near the ruins of an abandoned factory on the outskirts of Geneva. We had escaped Kaveh, but barely. The Sovereign Order wasn't going to let us slip away again.

Esha shivered, wringing water from her hair. "Well, that went spectacularly wrong."

Rohan collapsed onto the ground, groaning. "I think my spleen is somewhere back in the river. If anyone finds it, please return it."

Bilal cracked his neck. "We should keep moving. Kaveh isn't dead, and the Order will track us soon."

I pulled out the flash drive, gripping it tightly. "We have one shot at this. We need to take the fight to them—before they finish what they started."

Esha glanced at the city skyline. "Then we need firepower. And I know just the place."

Lock and Load

The weapons cache was hidden in the basement of an old nightclub—one of Esha's many questionable contacts had stashed it years ago. The place reeked of stale beer and bad decisions.

Rohan whistled, admiring the arsenal. "Wow. This is either really impressive or very illegal."

Esha smirked. "Can't it be both?"

Bilal checked a sniper rifle, nodding in approval. "This will do. We'll need explosives too. Kaveh won't go down easy."

I strapped on a bulletproof vest, rolling my shoulders. "We don't walk away from this fight. Either we take the Order down, or they bury us."

Rohan sighed. "Ah, a classic 'all or nothing' scenario. Just once, I'd like a mission where we get to retire peacefully on a beach."

Esha tossed him a grenade. "You can take this to the beach if it makes you feel better."

With weapons in hand, we made our way to the Order's command center—a heavily fortified estate on the outskirts of Geneva. If Kaveh was still alive, this was where he'd be waiting.

Bilal hacked into their security grid, disabling the outer defenses. "We have ten minutes before they realize we're here."

Rohan grinned, checking his rifle. "Then let's make them count."

The first explosion rocked the compound, sending guards into chaos. Esha took out the snipers while I led the charge through the front gates.

Bullets tore through the air as we fought our way inside. The Order wasn't prepared for an attack this bold.

Kaveh appeared at the top of the stairs, his face bruised but his smirk intact. "I was hoping you'd come back, Ahaan. Let's finish this."

I raised my gun. "Gladly."

135

The Showdown

The fight with Kaveh was brutal. He moved like a phantom, dodging my strikes and countering with deadly precision. But this time, I wasn't fighting alone.

Esha flanked him, landing a brutal kick to his ribs. Rohan fired, forcing him back. Bilal took out the remaining guards, covering our escape route.

Kaveh wiped blood from his lip, laughing. "You really think killing me will stop the Order? We are everywhere. Cut off the head, and another takes its place."

I pulled out the flash drive. "Not this time. We're exposing everything. The world will know."

Kaveh's smile faltered. For the first time, he looked afraid.

I fired.

Kaveh staggered back, clutching his chest. His body hit the ground.

Silence.

Esha exhaled. "Is he finally dead?"

Rohan nudged him with his foot. "Yeah, pretty sure. But let's not stick around to find out."

We uploaded the Order's files to every major news outlet in the world. Within hours, governments were in chaos, scrambling to deal with the fallout. The Sovereign Order was no longer a secret.

Bilal watched the news broadcast, shaking his head. "We did it."

I nodded. "Yeah. We did."

Rohan raised a bottle of whiskey. "To not dying. Barely."

Esha smirked. "And to making the world a little less corrupt."

We clinked glasses, the weight of our victory finally sinking in. The war was over.

Or so we thought.

Because somewhere in the shadows… a new enemy was waiting.

Epilogue: Shadows And Echoes

The world had changed overnight. The Sovereign Order, once untouchable, was now the subject of international investigations. Arrests were being made, assets seized. Their network was crumbling.

And yet, I couldn't shake the feeling that we had only cut off a limb, not the head.

We were holed up in a safehouse in Amsterdam, watching the news cycle repeat our victory. Rohan poured another drink, stretching his sore muscles. "So, this is what winning feels like? Not bad. Not great, but not bad."

Esha rolled her eyes. "It's not over. There are still people out there who want to rebuild the Order. Someone will take Kaveh's place."

Bilal leaned against the window, silent for a moment. "We've done something no one else could. We brought them into the light. Now it's up to the world to decide what happens next."

I exhaled, watching the city lights. "And what happens to us?"

Rohan smirked. "Well, I vote for a long vacation. Preferably on a beach, with no explosions."

Esha snorted. "Give it a week before you get bored and start chasing bad guys again."

A knock at the door made us all freeze. No one was supposed to know we were here.

I reached for my gun, signaling for silence. Slowly, I opened the door.

A man stood there, his face hidden in the dim light. He slid an envelope into my hand and spoke only one sentence before vanishing into the night.

"You think it's over? You're just getting started."

I looked down at the envelope, my fingers trembling as I opened it. Inside was a single photograph.

Kaveh. Alive.

Smiling.

The war wasn't over.

It was just beginning.

Afterword

Writing, The Sovereign Files has been an incredible journey. This story began as a simple idea— a luxurious trip, and evolved into something deeply horrid. Ahaan's journey mirrors the struggles many of us face when choosing between whom to believe, what to believe.

I hope this book has resonated with you in some way. Whether it reminded you of a murder mystery or an action-packed thriller, the magic of handwritten letters, or the courage it takes to start over, I am grateful you shared this journey with me.

With gratitude,
Agnith Banerjee